Seers

Seers

a novel by KRISTINE BOWE

To Kyle, who knows how to celebrate small wins like big victories

Seers
Text Copyright © 2013 Kristine Bowe

A Mackinac Island Book
Published by Charlesbridge
85 Main Street
Watertown, MA 02472
(617) 926-0329
www.charlesbridge.com

Library of Congress Cataloging-in-Publication Data
Bowe, Kristine.
    Seers / Kristine Bowe.
        p. cm.
    Summary: Teenager Elise Felton is both a "seer" and an "extractor", someone who can penetrate another person's memories and remove them, and she believes that by working with her mentor Tobias she will be able to recover her own memories, but Tobias has plans of his own.
    ISBN 978-1-934133-55-2 (reinforced for library use)
    ISBN 978-1-934133-56-9 (softcover)
    1. Telepathy—Juvenile fiction. 2. Memory—Juvenile fiction. 3. Ethical problems—Juvenile fiction. 4. Conspiracies—Juvenile fiction. [1. Telepathy—Fiction. 2. Memory—Fiction. 3. Ethics—Fiction. 4. Conspiracies—Fiction.] I. Title.
    PZ7.B6719432See 2013
    813.6--dc23   2013008808

Printed April 2013 by Worzalla Publishing Company in Stevens Point, Wisconsin, USA
(hc) 10 9 8 7 6 5 4 3 2 1
(sc) 10 9 8 7 6 5 4 3 2 1

Mackinac Island Press
for the love of reading

Chapter

"Your ID card, please. Miss? Do you have your ID card? Miss? Your *card*?"

I come out of it. I am in the office of my new school. My third high school in the past year.

The way she spit out that last word brought me out of it. I hadn't been watching or listening or even present, for that matter, but I guess by the look on her face that her questions started out much less curt than she sounded just now.

"I'm sorry, I . . . here." I fumble with my wallet and ease out my school ID. She purposely keeps her eyes lowered as she reaches for it. A trick I use as well. A power play. No eye contact. Her allowing me to smile or sweetly plead with my eyes or make some pathetic face for her to see would be her allowing me to make amends. She clearly isn't in a forgiving mood and isn't going to give me the opportunity. Fine by me. I don't want to pretend to care that I held up the nonexistent line behind me or kept her from another doughnut or cup of coffee or from her doodling or texting or whatever else she does to not work at work.

"Wait here. I'll print your schedule." Her voice is more even now. She isn't pursing her lips as much. She must be telling herself that I am just a teenager and should not be expected to know how to act. She may be mellowing, but I am revving up.

Wait here? Where am I going to go? Shall I simply pick a class at the end of the hall and hope I'm interested in the lesson? Hope it's not something I've already been taught? Sure. I'll wait here for a schedule of classes I don't care to attend.

The secretary waddles back, and as she hands me my list of assignments, I notice how the ring on her pointer finger is wedged on so tight that it pinches back the fat like a dam staving off rising water. I can't hold back any longer. Get a bigger ring. Get your roots done. Get fewer chins. As I try to decide what it is about this woman that has made me feel as if my gut is boiling, I go in.

Typical brown. Nothing special. No over-activity. No under-activity. Average. Boring. Unfulfilled professionally. Insecure physically. Likes to knit. Knit? Seriously? There's nothing here. Wait . . . adopted. Interesting. Why? Foster care until age thirteen. Thirteen? That's old to still be in the system. She must have been a special teenager, a good kid, to have been adopted that old without all the cuteness of a toddler, the rosy cheeks and all. She must know what it's like to move a lot, what it's like to be a new kid. I rub my hands over the memory. High-school graduate. Wife. Mother. Now grandmother. Back to boring. I'm leaving.

When I come back, she is staring at me, of course. I am used to this by now. I glance at my schedule and then look at her. She allows me this time to look her in the eyes. By now she thinks my spacing out may be due to anxiety or social ineptness caused by moving around a lot, and now she is connected to me. Because she moved around a lot, too. And now she wonders about my parents. She wonders if I have the instability she had. She hopes I find the settling down she found. She *wants* me to be happy. She *needs* me to be happy. Because the memory I rubbed a second ago is fresh for her now.

"I hope you have a good day, dear." Her lips turn up in a half smile. She is secure in her feelings for me but unsure of my response. Do I forgive her for her tone earlier? Do I understand that she was just frustrated? How was she to know that I was just nervous and not one of the tons of insubordinate, ill-mannered punks she has to manage every day?

"I hope you have a good day, too. Thanks for all your help." I even smile.

Her eyes twinkle. Well, the one I went in does. She is relieved. She would have felt badly all day had I not shown her my acceptance and made her feel as if my transition as the new kid has been made easier thanks to the help of the school secretary.

I don't enjoy the easy ones anymore.

Chapter

A Seer is like a mind reader, you could say. A mind reader can hear thoughts, so in the moment, being a mind reader is useful. If you want to know who in the room finds you ridiculously attractive, read minds. If you want to know what the catty girls are squealing about behind your back that second, read their minds. What play are they running? How should I line up my defense? Sure. Read on. Win the game.

But minds change, don't they? Monday a girl hates my outfit. Tuesday she wishes she had my figure. If I read her mind on Monday, she's on my list. But I probably won't ever wear that ensemble again. Tuesday, though, I have no time for her. Why bother? She already wants to be me. What else can I win?

Mind readers can change their reactions to people or the way people react toward them by gaining privileged information and using it to their advantage. It would be comforting to know that you can be sure of your acceptance by others. Never again would you have to rely on body language, eye contact, facial expressions, or the like. You would undoubtedly know. Yes. The popular kids do think you're cool. No. Not cool enough to be accepted into their clique. No. He isn't going to call. Yes. He does just want to be friends.

But a Seer travels into a being's brain. It's not just about thoughts with a Seer. Thoughts are the key, but not all. A Seer determines not only what the being is thinking but also how deeply that being *can* think. The more intelligent the being, the deeper the thoughts. Sometimes the depth of thought is innocent, sometimes for the good of us all, and sometimes not.

First we assess basic brain function and capacity. How smart. How dumb. Healthy. Sick.

Then we assess activities and interests. Then past experiences, memories. And motivations. Motivations to cure. Motivations to kill. And everything in between.

We can enter a being's brain at will. At our choosing. It doesn't happen upon contact. It is a forced action. Like choosing to open and walk through a door. We don't have unlimited time in, though, and it is taxing, so we choose our doors carefully. We don't like to waste trips, Tobias says. We must show restraint, Tobias says. We must always remember our path, Tobias says. I tend to be a tad liberal with my traveling. I have what Tobias calls "problems with restraint and lack of temper management."

Tobias is my Preceptor, or my mentor. I document my experiences as a Seer in a daily journal and meet with him every evening. He helps guide my future Navigations and choices. He says there is something off about the way I Navigate. Something off about the way I See.

Tobias says that Seers are born with their ability. They can be Seers on their own, without a Preceptor. But although Seers without a Preceptor may travel into their friends, family members, or other people with whom they come into contact, they will not develop their abilities. They will not master their skills or be placed on missions for the good of all Seers and humans alike. They are the recreational. We, those with Preceptors, are the Navigational.

As Navigational Seers age, a desire begins to well up in them. They begin to feel as if they belong somewhere, with someone, though they do not know why. They begin to make moves toward connecting with that someone. That someone is their Preceptor. They have an unspoken connection, like a signal. It will continue to grow in strength as the Seer ages. The signal will build in strength as the Seer nears its source, but a Seer needs time to find and move toward that connection. Seers will naturally and unknowingly travel toward their Preceptor until a Preceptor finds them.

I imagine it being like the way mosquitos find even a bare inch of flesh. How do they find me so fast? Didn't I just step outside? Yet there they are. I watch them hover over my exposed thigh, closing in and retreating, closing in and retreating, until finally, contact. How must their urge and desire feel to them that they simply cannot keep themselves from finding me, from connecting? Did I hover around Tobias for a while before I landed?

Tobias says that without a Preceptor, a Seer will never fully develop his or her talents because it is the Preceptor who acts as a guardian in the place of the Seer's family, arranges the missions, and helps the Seer to find his or her special skills.

By the age of seven, the strongest Seers have found the scent, followed the path, and found their Preceptor. By the age of seven, the urge, the desire, has become too strong to resist. They cannot help but to make contact. Children as young as three have been known to maneuver their way to their Preceptor. Some by coincidence. Some by choice. Preceptors believe that a Seer's mere presence in the family can influence parents' decisions about where they choose to live. Parents move to a new town. The preschool is next to a regional headquarters. Bam. Connection. I've been told that some young Seers, the ones with the strongest senses, the most skill, have left a playground, climbed a fence, or jumped from a moving vehicle to get to their Preceptor. These are usually the ones who will one day become Preceptors themselves. Tobias says that connecting with one's Preceptor is the only way to ensure that a Seer will truly master his or her talents and find the right missions, missions that showcase the Seer's strengths, missions that make a difference.

And then there's me. I was seventeen.

I remember how much I learned at my first meeting with Tobias. Tobias is a sound teacher with vast knowledge of the Seers' organization and the nature of Seers' abilities. But unfortunately, his knowledge about me is minimal. I showed up at his door almost a year ago. The address of the headquarters must have been lonely floating around in my brain by itself. Because my brain was an empty shell. I have been tested and drilled and tested again. But no one can tell me where my memories are, why they were taken, or what exactly my life consisted of before Tobias.

Tobias told me that Seers rely on sound to travel in. They ride in on a wave, as they say. A sound wave. They concentrate on the vibrations in the being's voice or the sound it's making, then

7

close their eyes and ride the wave in through the ear. Imagine a storm cloud, a twister. The Seer's ear a twister, the being's ear a twister. Water in between. The being's sound in the Seer's ear creates its own storm, and the Seer rides the wave through the water into the next twister, the being's ear. I picture it gray with white, foamy, angry crests on the tips of the waves. Gray clouds. Rumbling thunder as the sound becomes existence itself. Swirling. Churning. Gliding. Sliding. Like a water slide. Only I hate water slides. I hate angry waves. And I hate ears. They're ugly.

I go in through the eye.

Chapter

3

Schedule in hand, I walk down the E corridor to my first class. E corridor is senior hall. I am technically a senior. By age. By credits. But since I have been to so many high schools, I am a senior with no ties, no tearful good-byes looming in the near future. No favorite teachers, classes. No clique. No friends. All of those things, that feeling of belonging, would be possible if I were here as a normal student. But I'm not. And if all goes well, I will only be a senior here for a few weeks anyway.

My first class is physics. The door is closed. There is something far more invasive about entering a classroom full of strangers when the class has already begun if the door is closed. Somehow the door being open makes me feel as if they were expecting me or expecting anyone, for that matter. They are open to the possibility of it, at least. But a closed door screams, "We are full! Can you not see that we are not presently accepting guests?"

I turn the handle and sidestep in.

"May I help you?" asks the wiry-haired woman in the center of the room. She begins to weave through lab tables toward me. Her eyes, intently fixed on me, are small and glassy but somehow avoid the label *beady* and achieve *keen*. I don't have to Navigate her to See that her intelligence level is above average. Some people have lace curtains, sheer panels maybe, over their eyes. They give away so much of themselves without trying or even realizing it. Most people's eyes are shielded as if drapes made from stiff, heavy fabric hang behind them. They effectively keep their secrets to themselves. I've encountered only a few people who have room-darkening blinds drawn behind their eyes, and I can't tell a thing about them. This lady's eyes hide nothing.

"I'm new. I'm in this class," I say as I thrust my schedule at her as if I need to prove it.

"Happy to have you." She glances down and reads, "'Elise Felton.' Do you go by Elise?"

"Leesie, actually. Thanks." Most people don't ask. I hate having to broach the subject myself. It's such an easy thing to do, to ask what someone likes to be called. I wonder why it doesn't occur to more people. I instantly like her.

"I'm Mrs. Marion. We just started a new unit. The first and second laws of thermodynamics. Had you started thermodynamics in your previous school?"

Seriously? The study of the energy transfer between systems? Sounds like any day of my life.

"Yes, I have."

"Great!" She begins to turn away. I can tell that she needs to get back to the lesson. The class has been busily staring at me, but despite the new attraction, they're getting chatty and restless. "Grab a textbook from the shelf and a seat in the back." Then she addresses the class: "Class, this is Leesie Felton. Welcome her on her first day. Don't leave her stranded in the hallway if she looks lost and help her to the cafeteria! Let's continue."

I take notes the remainder of the period. It's quiet, and I feel safe in my seat. I am not looking forward to the hallway at the bell. I'll have to pretend to be secure and unassuming. Approachable but not needy. Confident but not overtly alluring. Interesting, not weird.

This is a jeans and T-shirt school. The style of the jeans doesn't seem to matter. I'm wearing dark jeans, plain, like half the girls. The other half wears a blend of colored, straight leg, ripped. Good. No fashion gurus spotted yet. I chose a gray shirt this morning, wanting to blend in. At least clothes-wise. There isn't much I can do about the rest of me.

A Preceptor in Tobias's building says my hair color is like the part of the fire where white flame and orange flame play over the coals. And that pretty much sums it up. I am walking fire with blondish-reddish, wavy hair sailing down my back. I send a chunk of it over my shoulder.

At the bell I take my time getting to the door.

"Hey. Can I help you get to your next class?" A boy is leaning against the doorframe. He's tall and lanky and looks smart. It's not the same way Mrs. Marion shows her brain's secrets with her easy-reader eyes. His is in his stance. It's in his speech. His stance is relaxed yet ready to pounce, and his words are chopped and crisp, like he's taking time to say them even though I can tell he must have an endless stream of words and thoughts swimming in his head. He has clear green eyes, and my guess is he considers himself somewhat representative of the student body, political even.

"Sure. Thanks." I hand him my schedule.

"Calculus. Good. Science and then math. That makes good sense. Mr. Stein. Good. This way."

He's funny to watch. Kind of bobble-heady as he agrees with himself. I especially love the way he doesn't look up to see if I agree as well. I follow him.

"I'm in one of your classes. AP English. We're studying British romanticism right now. You just missed the Restoration and the eighteenth century, but this is good, too."

This actually piques my interest. I love British literature. "Okay. I'll see you then. Thanks for getting me here."

"My pleasure. I'm Ryan, by the way."

"Nice to meet you, Ryan. Leesie."

"Right. Leesie. Got it. Bye." He gives a little wave and ducks into his class. It looks like a history class, from the posters.

Calculus goes the way you expect any math class to go. All business. Notes. Problems modeled by the teacher. Practice problems to try on your own. Practice problems review. More for homework. Nobody talks to me, which is fine. I am pleased so far with how easily my new fellow students are allowing me to fly under the radar.

The bell rings, and I see Ryan. Punctual. I'm not surprised. His notebooks are fresh and straight. He has a pen in his hand and a calculator in his pocket. This is a convenient guy to meet on the first day. A great study partner.

"How was calculus?" he asks.

I look at him to assess him before I answer. If he is looking down or away from me or fiddling with his books or checking his phone, he doesn't care about my answer. He is filling in time with pointless and meaningless conversation. Asking to say he asked. If he is looking at me, well, then I will say more than, "Fine." We make eye contact. He holds my gaze for a second, but then his eyes dart past me and down to his books and at the teacher coming our way. And then back at me.

Okay. So he cares enough to ask, but I'm not high on his list of priorities. Fine, Ryan. Good thing I'm not here for you.

"It was good, I think. Differentiation. I know a little about it already, so I think I'll be okay," I answer casually.

"I can help if you need it. Math is my forte." He smiles.

"I appreciate that. I may take you up on it. I'm looking forward to English, though. If *I* have a forte, that'd be it."

"Okay, then. Let me know if you need any help," Ryan says, this time looking directly at me. He shakes his head to the left, and I watch the wave of sandy brown hair readjust itself across his brow.

"Great, Ryan. Thanks."

His generosity could be useful. But only if he's in close contact with the one I'm here for.

Chapter

4

As I turn left onto Broad Street, following the signs for 295 North, which will get me out of New Jersey and into Philadelphia, I feel like Clark Kent stripping in the phone booth and emerging as Superman. I travel farther from my new school and from my guise as a regular student, toward Tobias and his office. I shed my regular girl thoughts of jeans and John Keats and ready my brain for the batch of information Tobias has for me today.

Tobias keeps close tabs on me. I live above his office, our area headquarters, in a studio apartment, so his access to me is easy. In addition to his regular checks, we have information sessions, where he tells me about the history of Seers and the organization, as well as mission meetings, where he provides me with insight into my mission subjects. Sometimes he shares what little he knows about my own backstory.

In the light, early-afternoon traffic, I make my way easily to the exit for the Ben Franklin Bridge. My mind wanders to a meeting with Tobias a few weeks ago when he drilled me on what I know about my past and had me recount a memory I retained. I shared the only one that I recall vividly.

My memories are like the silken threads of a cobweb—an old, dusty cobweb that has been reduced to only a few wisps. The strongest, longest of those wisps is the memory of my first

Extraction. This was the trip that changed the whole game for me. I knew by then that I could do something that no one else I knew could do. I figured that out on my own, as all Seers do But that day I knew that Navigating was for a purpose. That I could gain from it. That the being could lose from it. My first victim was Jennifer Dixon.

I had a friend named Sharon. Jennifer was her older sister. Jennifer was a formidable force. She hated our presence. We were little eight-year-olds who brought down the "coolness" that was her house. Sharon's parents were never home. Billy, the eighteen-year-old brother, was supposed to be in charge, but he couldn't be bothered. Jennifer, fourteen, did everything she could to remove Sharon and me from the scene so her friends could do what they wanted without the threat of being tattled on—which Sharon and I often did. But you couldn't blame us; Jennifer deserved everything she got. Everything.

On this day I remember, Jennifer was at her most lethal. She was awaiting the arrival of her popular-crowd cronies, and Sharon and I were doing the most heinous and embarrassing of things: standing in the kitchen, leaning on the counter, picking from a bowl of day-old popcorn. Jennifer didn't waste any time.

"The last thing you need is another calorie, Sharon. Didn't Mom tell you to cut back?" She sang the last sentence a little, and her words attacked Sharon the way a winter breeze bites your face if your nose is running and your eyes are tearing. Sharon's hand went immediately to her shirt. She pulled it out and adjusted it, a trick she'd recently begun to do whenever anyone looked at her directly. Sharon was chubby. She was made fun of at school, but I knew she was most uncomfortable at home.

My stomach began to churn and ache, and I clenched my teeth. My nostrils flared. I knew I was wearing the anger on my face. I knew I was glaring at Jennifer. She looked me in the eyes. She challenged me. She was convinced she could—would—win. I was just a kid. A dumb kid, to her. Dumb enough to be friends with her fat sister. I went in.

This time I traveled faster than usual. Grayish blue. Average. Properly functioning.

I swam through layers without bothering to properly assess. She was in working order. She was of average intelligence. So what? I was in here for something. What? What could I do to her in here that would hurt her? *Permanently.* Suddenly there was something purposeful about my trip.

Each layer has a general feeling to it. All beings give off a mood in each layer. It's like summing up a year of your life, the mood of that year of your life, in one or two words. Only you don't get to do it. I do. So if the mood that permeated a year of your life was loneliness, insecurity, rejection, you don't get to say "fulfilling" or "satisfying." There is no lying or hiding your true emotions or your deepest, darkest secrets when you don't even know I'm in your brain.

Usually an event, a single moment, will determine the emotion for the layer. People underestimate the power that hours, even minutes, play in shaping who they have become. A scene that plays out in an afternoon, an afternoon of hugs, kind words, beautiful weather, maybe a picnic, complete acceptance and security, can brand, say, a third-year layer "content." The more neutral or positive layers a being has, the more neutral or positive the being.

Jennifer's outer layers had been neutral. Where was her emotional gauge set? Why were there so many years set at neither good nor bad? Had nothing notable happened to her? Or had she put her guard up somewhere, at some layer, to protect herself? What had happened to her?

The angry, churning feeling in my gut was replaced by the feeling you get when you swing too high on the swings. That little ping—if it had a sound would sound like the one a tuning fork makes. Was that a feeling of concern? Was I *concerned* about Jennifer? Seriously? I hated her. I loathed her. I wanted her to trip up the steps while every boy in her school watched. I wanted to see her cry the way I had seen Sharon cry because of something terrible Jennifer said. Didn't I?

Sixth grade . . . neutral. Fifth grade: neutral/negative. Why? I went down another layer. I knew it would get worse farther down. Fourth grade: Negative. What was the word? What was the mood? It was murky. She wasn't clear water. She was a pond, an iced-tea brown. I knew that layers became cloudy when the being was working hard to forget a year. This was pretty murky. She was working hard to conceal whatever was here.

The word: *pretend*. Pretend? The whole layer was "pretend"? I had to go lower.

Third grade: negative. The word: *betrayed*.

It was a thicker muck in this layer. The layer had gone from iced tea to iced latte. Foamy and creamy. She worked daily, maybe even moment to moment, on keeping this layer churned up. She was not trying to forget this layer. She needed to forget this layer. This layer could break her, and she knew it.

The tuning fork feeling in my stomach was now a tuba blowing an endless low note. My eyes were burning, and I knew this meant I should bail. But what had happened to her? Who had betrayed her? I had to stay in this layer and look around. This was the key to why she always attacked Sharon. Why did she relentlessly spit hurtful words at her? Why did she want to dash Sharon's confidence so badly?

There was a thick whirlpool in front of me. I knew how to find it because I followed the cold.

"Keeping it on ice," as Seers say. It's amazing how many clichés mean a whole different thing to a Seer. When a being is repressing, hiding from, or blocking out a particular moment in a layer, the layer is noticeably colder than the one before it. It will be colder still and moving, usually churning, around the moment itself. This complicates my getting at the moment, of course. I tread in front of it, straining my arms. If I can fold my fingers in the direction of the whirlpool as it passes by my hands, I can enter it.

I felt the icy thickness pass my wrists. I cupped my fingers and propelled forward. I moved with the thickness and began to spin. By now my eyes had gone past burning to feeling as if someone had pinned my eyelids back and was raking my eyeballs with coarse sandpaper. I took a deep breath to readjust to the new pain level and hoped to find what I needed before it was too late.

The thickness now had chunks, rocks, globs, that I had to swim through. A rock of pure sadness, a glob of old tears and anger and pain hit me in the shin, and I knew I'd pay later for each hit I took. I surged to the right to avoid another and saw her.

A nine-year-old Jennifer. It was late afternoon. She was standing by the window at the front of the house. She was waiting for someone. Behind her sat a man in a swivel recliner that usually faced the TV. But it was now facing Jennifer. As she clutched the curtain, her shoulders heaved and shook. She'd been crying for some time. Her swollen eyes scanned the top of the hill for the promise of a friendly car coming to save her. Finally the familiar golden beige of the Buick descended.

Jennifer thrust the front door open and took the steps two at a time. Her mother had barely put the car in park before Jennifer was yanking at the door handle.

"Hold on, Jennie! Give me a minute! You're going to break the door. . . . Honey, you've been crying! What is it? What happened?

"I didn't mean to. I tried to do everything he told me to do. I was quiet. I cleaned up my messes. I only asked a question, Mom." Jennifer was spitting the words out as quickly as she could. Her mother needed to know how good she was. Her mother needed to know that she had followed all the rules, had eaten all her lunch, and had picked up her toys. She had only asked a question.

Another rock slammed me back. It hit me in the chest. They were getting bigger. Stronger. Angrier.

"What are you talking about? What happened?" Jennifer's mother's voice tightened. "Davis, what is she talking about?" She turned to her brother for answers. Davis had been babysitting that day while Jennifer's dad took Billy to the day camp where the boy was working and Jennifer's mom took Sharon to an event at the library.

"She's upset with me because I told her she couldn't have a snack. She had just eaten all her lunch. She had enough. She didn't need any more food. Other than that she was good. She's just upset—that's all." Davis watched Jennifer as he lied.

"Mom, that's not true. I mean, yes, I asked for a snack, but Davis hit me. Mom, he hit me." Jennifer's lip quivered, and her eyes pleaded. She had been waiting for her mom for so long. She needed to be held and told that it's okay. That she didn't do anything wrong. That she didn't have to be afraid anymore. Uncle Davis had never hit her before, had never raised his voice to her before. Though she had never been left alone with him before . . .

"What? Jennifer, come on. Uncle Davis wouldn't do that, honey." She turned to him. "Davis?"

"Of course I didn't hit her! I pushed her hand away from the snack drawer. A nudge! Honestly, Sue. She eats too much. I was just trying to help her to pace herself. Really, she had just eaten lunch." He avoided Jennifer's gaze now. He seemed to be looking everywhere else.

"Jenn. Honey. You know I've talked to you about waiting a while in between meals for a snack, and what were you asking for? Junk? Please. And Uncle Davis was nice enough to stay with you today. You shouldn't make up stories like this!"

Jennifer slumped forward. Her body had been poised for embrace, for her mother to wrap her up and squeeze her in, and tell her that no one had the right to put his hands on her, that she didn't deserve the back-handed slap Uncle Davis had used to bat her away from the snack drawer, that she didn't eat too much, that she looked just fine, and that everything would be okay now because Mom was here.

And now a whole new level of betrayal.

Mom? You don't believe me? She couldn't bring herself to say the words aloud. She couldn't bear to hear her mother's answer aloud. She had no confidence left. She had never imagined that she wouldn't be believed. She had worried that her mother might not approve of her snacking; that had become the norm lately. Jennifer had always been encouraged to eat, to finish her plate, praised when she did, and then always offered seconds. But this year . . .

She felt so unworthy, so pathetic, so betrayed. She had learned in a single moment that she didn't always rank. That she wasn't always heard. That she was fat.

In that moment Jennifer's mother ripped out a part of her that left a gaping hole. The mistreatment by Uncle Davis was hurtful. No one wants to be physically attacked for wanting something to eat. But for her mother to back him up? Devastating. For her mother to believe Uncle Davis? It ranked her below her uncle. It stripped her of the idea that she had a parent who would ride in on a flaming chariot to save her. She must have been crushed. She must have chosen every word carefully from that point on. She must have watched every mouthful. It must have shaped the way she behaved.

Fourteen-year-old Jennifer hardly ate. Her hip bones jutted out of her low-rise jeans. She was obsessed with the way she looked and seemed fidgety and self-conscious around her mother. The way Sharon was fidgety and self-conscious in front of Jennifer. Did chubby eight-year-old Sharon just remind Jennifer too much of herself at this layer? Could she not help but to belittle Sharon the way she was belittled at that age? Did she even know why she did it? Was it beyond her power to stop?

Usually at this point, I'd close my eyes and leave. I had the information. I knew why Jennifer hated Sharon. Jennifer *was* Sharon, and in every moment Jennifer was around Sharon, she was reminded of the pain she felt that day, the day her uncle, her mother, and her own body became her enemies.

But something had happened to me while I was fighting to stay in, fighting for this memory, fighting for Sharon. It hit me that maybe I was able to do more than travel into a being's brain. Maybe I could maneuver or manipulate the memories. As I veered left and right to avoid the masses of tangled tears and pain, I wanted to defend myself. I wanted to throw something, kick something, and tear something apart. No. The idea of an attack wasn't it. There was something else I needed to do.

For the first time, I felt this overwhelming desire well up inside me. I wanted to do more than know what was at the core of Jennifer's troubles. I wanted to *take* something. I wanted to grab at something that would end the struggle. For *Sharon*. But what? I had to grab at something that would end the whirlpool of hurt and muck and at the same time change life for Jennifer and Sharon. Could I do that? If I could feel the assault of Jennifer's repressions, feel them hit me and send me reeling, then I could touch, grasp, and pull something out with me. Couldn't I?

I reached out and down, back to the center of the revolving brown sludge. My icy fingers would barely bend in response to my commands, and I fumbled for a second before I felt anything. And then I was there. At the car. The three of them were there.

I extended my hands as I neared them. I passed Jennifer. I passed Uncle Davis. I was taking the mother.

I curled my fingers past her shoulders and around her collarbone. I dug into the flesh beneath and used it as a handle as I yanked her upward. Her head slumped forward, chin on her chest. I stared down at the top of her mother's head and flailing feet as we sailed upwards. She looked and felt real, and yet I knew I was holding on to an image burned into Jennifer's memory. I was *holding* an image. The magnitude of what I had discovered began to set in. I could control a memory. I could alter a layer of a being's life. If only I knew what this would do to Jennifer. How would it change her?

I had removed her mother from the moment. To Jennifer, only the memory of her uncle would persist. She would continue to hate him. She had been betrayed by him. He had made her feel judged, unloved, fat. But her mother had not. Her mother was not at the car. The details of the rest of that day would be fuzzy. Jennifer would not remember how the incident had been resolved. She would just know that she had moved past it enough not to continue to dwell on every detail of that day. Jennifer would be able to see her mother and feel safe and accepted. She could see Sharon and not feel reminded of hurt and betrayal.

I snapped back to my travels as a new level of pain I had yet to experience reminded me that I had to get out of there. I had never been in for so long. Suddenly I was aware of the flames that seemed to be roaring in my eye sockets. My legs were heavy. My arms ached, and my fingers screamed for me to dislodge them from their collarbone prison. But I held on. I pulled Jennifer's mother up with me through the layers. My once-sharp view of these neutral layers was replaced by a red haze that seemed to be getting thicker. The red haze parted a bit. I could see the cloud-like film of Jennifer's outer layer that I needed to swim to and break through. The top of my head touched first. As soon as I felt contact, I closed my eyes. I was out.

Jennifer's mother disappeared from my hands. I panicked at first. What had I done? Common sense kicked in, and I reasoned that once I removed her from her space in Jennifer's third-grade layer, she wouldn't exist in that state anywhere else. Members in a memory have a specific age, haircut, outfit, facial expression, and feeling attached to them. Jennifer's mother was only in her memory looking as she did and behaving exactly as she did in that layer. I hadn't erased her mother completely or harmed her or Jennifer in any way. Jennifer would be able to reshape her opinion of herself and her relationship with her mother now that her mother hadn't betrayed her by siding with

Uncle Davis. Her mother hadn't agreed that Jennifer was a liar or fat and disgusting and that it was okay to be slapped if she tried to eat something. Only Uncle Davis had done that. And maybe that was damaging. And maybe that would explain her obsession with weight and her looks, but she would still have her mother by whom she could feel loved and accepted and could have a general feeling of self-worth. And she wouldn't hate and want to attack Sharon.

I had never felt such intense burning. I pinched my eyes closed, but that only added a dull aching in my head to the burn.

I Navigate with my eyes open. I stare into the eye of my target, feel myself—my soul, I guess—surge up through my body, foamy and frothy and whirling like cotton candy around the dome as it's tricked into spinning around the maker's stick. Only I flow out and into the eye I have chosen. In and down, starting at the most recent layer and traveling as far as I need to go. When I have to leave, I head back up the layers. When I reach the edge of the top layer, I close my eyes, and I am out.

I can't get past the burning because I am human, despite my abilities, and when you keep your eyes open too long, they burn. I can't close my eyes once I am in unless I'm at the top layer and touching the barrier. It's why my time is limited once I am in. It had never been a problem before. I could leave whenever I wanted. I would just go in, find out some things, surf around, and leave. But in Jennifer's brain, when I knew I had to find something, to fix someone, to take something out, the hazard of damaging my eyes in the process because I stayed in too long was the price I would pay until I could master the skill and get faster.

"What the . . . ? Oh, my God!" Jennifer was shrieking, and she and Sharon were spitting a string of incoherent half questions at me in pitches higher than I had ever heard their voices reach.

I just wanted them to shut up long enough for me to finish nursing my eyes. I was rubbing them, but it wasn't helping. I wasn't ready to open them. I was scared to open them. If they were burning this badly closed, could I bear to expose them to the air again?

"Leesie! What is wrong with you? Oh, God! You're *bleeding*!"

The crazed tone of Sharon's voice cut through the pain, and her stupid, high-pitched whining thrust me back to the moment. I pulled my hands away from my eyes and jerked them open. The first thing I saw was a red haze. Was I still in? This was the same haze from the last few layers of Jennifer. As my vision cleared and my eyes adjusted, I saw the outline of my fingers and the blood that was on them. Not red haze. Blood. What was bleeding? My *eyes* were bleeding? I had known time was limited. I had experienced bloodshot eyes and soreness that would persist even hours after I'd been in, but blood? I knew I had pushed it. And now I knew that working through the pain would get me nothing but two bloody eyes.

"Will you two shut up!" I have such a delicate way with people when they are emotional.

"Just get me a wet paper towel or something and stop screaming already! I'm fine!"

"Fine?" Sharon's voice was still pinched and squeaky. "Fine?

Your eyes are bleeding!"

"I am aware of that. Thanks."

Talking to them with my eyes closed and pinned behind bloody fingers while I waited for the wet paper towel was annoying me enough that I knew I had to watch what I said. I was two seconds from telling these two exactly where to stick it. And where was that *paper towel*?

Paper towel ripping. Water running. Finally.

"Here!" Sharon sounded wounded. And angry. . . . Was she angry? Great. Now I had to sound soothing and appreciative of all the concern. Who was bleeding here? Why must I cater to the frailty of the emotional gauges of others?

"Thanks. I'm okay. Really. I'm sorry. This just happens sometimes. It's no big deal," I said, thinking ahead as I was speaking. "Uh, I have enlarged blood vessels in my eyes. I was . . . born with it. Sometimes it flares up. Dry days . . . ."

Was today a dry day?

"Too cold, too hot, if I get a fever. Tons of triggers for it." I had better just leave the causes for spontaneous eye bleeding open-ended.

"You never told me," a miniature version of Sharon's voice piped in. She was hurt.

"I know. It's just weird to talk about. I guess I hoped you'd never see it." This softened her. I was attempting to get her to pity me for being a freak. It worked.

"No, I'm sorry! I'm so sorry you have to go through this! Does it hurt?"

Sharon really was so much nicer than I am. But this was

dragging on. I had to know what my pulling Mommy Dearest out of Jennifer's darkest moment in her most negative layer was going to do.

"It hurts. Yes. Let's just sit down. Jennifer, can you bring me a glass of water and maybe the popcorn over?" I was baiting her. Would she wait on us? Would she hand Sharon food without saying anything, or would she bail out of here as quickly as possible?

"Yeah, of course! I can't believe this. I've never heard of anything like this happening to anyone. How many times has this happened to you?" Her eyes were wide with concern. She put the glass in front of me, the popcorn in front of Sharon, and sat down in the chair next to her sister. She reached her hand into the popcorn bowl as Sharon's hand slipped in. They bumped knuckles as they each grabbed a handful. I couldn't see much through a thinning, though still present, red haze, but I could see changes. Definite changes. I could change brains.

I come out of this memory and change lanes, shifting to the right to turn onto Girard Avenue. I parallel park my truck on the side street that flanks the headquarters. The enormity of what I discovered the day I Navigated Jennifer is sprawled out in my head. Before I turn the handle to the building's side door, I pull my shoulders back and take a deep breath, attempting to clear my head or at least to tidy it. I tuck the Jennifer memory to the side so that I can focus on the current state of my brain and on what Tobias will lay out for me today.

Chapter

My daily meetings and first week at Alsinboro Academy go quickly and without incident. I cause little stir, which is my main priority. Not only do I not like gushing or probing attention, but I can't afford it. If I am to have a successful mission, I must blend in and form the necessary friendships.

Ryan is not necessary, but he is a welcome companion. In the span of a week, he has served as a study partner, lunch buddy, and hallway companion. His brain is so sharp. I can only estimate his IQ or what he would look like inside if I Navigated him, but I am sure his intellect would be among the highest I have seen. I was not surprised to meet someone of Ryan's intelligence at a high school for the intellectually gifted.

Alsinboro Academy is located in Preston, New Jersey, a mini-city about fifteen miles south of Philadelphia. Up to this point I have been handling only city missions. The city offers a constant stirring up that I find comforting. It mirrors my ever-changing lifestyle. With each new mission comes a new school, new group of friends, new conquest. With each section of Philly comes a new style. The storefronts change from brick colonials and brownstones, to the Liberty Bell and Betsy Ross's House, to glass and metal structures that scream space-age technology. I see familiar faces on certain streets, of course, but that isn't the focus in a big city. The focus is on the location, the action, the culture. Small suburbs focus on the family.

I had shuddered at the thought of suburbia. How could I go from the progressive hustle of the city to the uptight manicured lawns of South Jersey? I thought of weeping cherry trees on streets named Poplar Drive or Evergreen Avenue or Progress Boulevard (all actual names of streets near the academy). I thought of soccer moms and kids walking the dog, family bike rides down to the lake (of course there's a neighborhood lake, complete with ducks and a fountain, a walking bridge, and people fishing and kayaking). I thought of neighborhood picnics, the farm stand in town, and the fact that families would be old Preston families, staying generation after generation. What kind of spell does South Jersey cast? No one seems to move out of here. They certainly continue to move in, though.

Case in point: me. Because of the academy's reputation, the town is fairly used to newcomers, transfer students in search of a résumé builder. Had I been going to the public high school, my arrival would have raised more curiosity. What street do you live on? Play any sports? Drama club, maybe? What do your parents do? Are they interested in joining the historical society? I would be seen as a soon-to-be Preston lifer, instead of a smart kid making a pit stop before college.

Still, I'm sure everyone wonders why a student would change schools senior year, but no one has asked yet. Of course I have my answers ready to go. Tobias always provides me with a tight backstory. To me, Tobias is my Preceptor. To the world, he is my legal guardian, and he handles all of the necessary arrangements as I transfer from school to school. My missions primarily take place in high schools. After this school year I'll graduate to college and university locations and wherever I can phase in as a new entry-level hire. My missions usually take time because I have to form relationships, enough to know what it is I need to take out with me before I can effectively Navigate. I have to know the beings well enough to know the root of their emotional or psychological weakness. In other words, I must study the movements of my prey before I attack.

Today I will make contact with my target. She is in two of my classes: European history and studio art. Studio art is mingling-friendly and offers plenty of chances to strike up conversation. I have it at the end of the day. I muddle through note-taking, theorems, an author study on Elizabeth Gaskell, and lunch with Ryan and a few others from English class. Finally, art.

She's sitting at a four-seater table near the middle of the room. Ironic, I think. She's the middle of everything, it seems. She's not too smart to be approachable. She's not on the bottom rung, though. She's involved in theater but not as the lead. She's on the math and science panel that competes in academic bowls around the country; she puts on a solid show but doesn't carry the team. She is beautiful, but not in an off-putting way. She's even average height. Thin but not too thin. Hair medium length. *Come on, man. What sets you apart?* She's half Japanese. I guess there's that. But this is a pretty diverse school, so even that doesn't do much to single her out. I have a bio on her. I've done my homework, but all I know is her demographic. Everything else I need I will get only when I can convince her to trust me.

We're in the middle of a project, so everyone is walking around, gathering supplies, and picking up where they left off the day before. She has her paints in front of her and seems to be studying her piece, asking it what to do next.

"Eri?"

She looks up at me, slowly, painfully taking her eyes away from her work. I can see it won't be easy to get her to talk.

"Yes?"

"Hi. I'm Leesie. Do you mind if I set up here?" It's not a conspicuous request, considering that there are no unoccupied tables left. And since I'm new, my table hopping won't raise any red flags. She'll assume that I am searching for the location in the room that best fosters my creative genius or something.

"Hi. Uh, sure. No problem." She smiles at me to convince me further that she is willing to share and slides her paints and brushes to her left. I sit across from her. Since we're still in the set-up-and-decide-what-to-do stage, this may be my only opportunity to talk.

"So do you live in town?" Lame. But at least it requires an answer.

"Huh? Oh, yes. I do. On Delaware Ave. Right down the street. You? Did you just move to town?"

I know the sprawling homes right down the street. The stone and brick homes with wrap-around front porches, canvas awnings, and slate walkways.

"No. I commute. From the city."

Short, clipped answers. I have to trick her into thinking she initiated this conversation. Leave her wanting the information.

"The city! That's a drive. And the traffic! How long does it take you to get here?" I can see I have become at least moderately interesting to her.

"Twenty minutes with no traffic. With traffic? An hour was the longest so far."

"Wow. Well, you better get the most of the education, I guess. If you're gonna fight the traffic to get here." There's an "I have to get to work" tone to her voice that warns me this may be all I get today. I can't leave it at general politeness, though, because too many days of that and she labels me an acquaintance for good. I'm supposed to be making this girl my closest friend. I've got to get into her house. I've got to get into her head.

"I'm sure I will. Do *you* think you are?"

Direct questions that not only ask someone's opinion but also require self-assessment and self-discovery are uncommon, come by surprise, and are usually intriguing. It's not every day that someone asks how you are being directly affected by something in your life. I usually get asked about the weather.

"Do I think I'm getting a good enough education? Um . . . wow. I think so. I mean, yeah. The teachers are great. It's all AP, so we'll have plenty of college credits when we graduate. And the academy has a strong reputation . . . if we want to go to an Ivy League." She fidgets in her seat.

Such a politically correct answer. Ladies and gentlemen, may I present the next Miss America.

"But you," I say, continuing to probe her, "do you think you'll look back and know that you got everything you could get out of high school when you had the chance? Do you think we can know something like that as we sit in the moment?"

I'm looking directly at her now. We're not setting up our supplies anymore. The rest of the class has settled in to their individual projects. Only a few murmurs can be heard coming from the back of the room. She stops fidgeting, sits forward, puts both elbows on the table, and rests her chin on her hands. Her eyes meet mine. She is looking for motive. Why is this new girl asking me to think about my life? Why should I tell her? What is she after?

I can feel her searching me. Searching my eyes. I don't have to worry about what she will find. She's making sure she is not being played with. Sometimes the most inquisitive people ask the deepest of questions to hear themselves ask them, or better yet, in the hopes that others around hear them ask thought-provoking questions and think, *What a deep person! I wish I were that smart.* You know how you spot those people? Watch their faces as you attempt to answer that deep question that made you excited, that made you think your intelligence was being respected in that very moment because someone wanted, really wanted, to know your innermost thoughts and beliefs. But the truth is they get off on the delivery alone. They ask questions like that to see the excited and magnetic response they can get from people. And when you answer them? You can actually see their eyes glaze over as they wait for you to finish talking, so they can ask or say something else that will bring them even more attention. She won't find that on my face, in my eyes. I truly want to know her. I *need* to know her. And I can see that she believes me.

Eri furrows her brow and takes a deep breath. "No."

"No, we can't know something like that as we sit in the moment?"

"No. Not that. I think we know when we're not getting all we can get from something," she says in a hushed voice. Her eyes are soft. A deep brown like a fawn. "I mean, no, I'm not getting all that I can get from this place."

This place? Miss America just lost a point during the interview round. She also just became interesting. Let the game begin.

Chapter

6

With a first, semi-successful connection made with Eri, I can officially kick-start this mission. Tobias says missions will help me piece together the years of my life that I have lost. The space around the few memories I have left is cloudy and thick. I try to wade through it, but I get all turned around inside my own head and end up right back where I started. Tobias says that's why I have to be so careful. Probably why he's so protective, always watching. Because I didn't forget my past. Someone or something took my past, took my memories from me.

Tobias has provided me with as much information as he's been able to gather. He reasons that whoever attacked my brain and stole my memories also planted a memory of the headquarters building, of his address. I don't remember the day I showed up there. I own the memories from the day after my connection with Tobias until now. Except for the clear memory of my first Extraction, I see my memories through a gray haze, and some are filled with gaps and don't make sense to me.

Tobias says that to have any hope of regaining my past, I must focus on missions. A Seer's memory becomes more powerful as Navigational skills improve. And so each mission is more difficult. Tobias says it's like training for cross-country. You build up to your longest distance over time. The hope is that over time and after more missions, I may gain a better view of the spaces around my remaining memories and in that space, maybe even find more.

Since I found Tobias, nearly a year ago, I have completed four missions. Sometimes the mission's goal is to save, sometimes to defeat. Either way each mission is set up the same: enter an environment, form the necessary relationships, establish trust, gain entry, and Navigate to read or manipulate. Extract if necessary. My first mission was to gain entry into the aunt of a missing child. The family believed that this woman not only knew where the child was but was also responsible for her disappearance. They were right. For that mission I attended the high school of the aunt's daughter, befriended her, and found out how she felt about her mother. Then I gained access into their home. During a dinner with her family, I went in.

Since that first mission, I have Navigated a teenager's suicidal brother, an orphan to find clues as to how she became an orphan and if and where there were any living relatives, and the mother of a girl addicted to drugs. I don't exactly pass out candy canes at Christmas or paint the rainbows after a storm, but at least sometimes the result of my Navigation is positive. Now the sister knows how to help her brother. The orphan knows she is alone in this world; she won't waste her time wondering. And the mother will no longer see her daughter abuse herself with drugs because I found the layer of hurt that the mother had inflicted upon her daughter, and I took it.

My missions are always unique in that I have to form background knowledge in order to Navigate. Because I have to get to know the beings, each mission has its own backstory. If

I wasn't going in to retrieve or change something, I could go in cold. I could find out where my target was in that moment, show up there, make eye contact, and dive in. But what would I be looking for? What single memory would change lives in a way that would complete my mission? Other Seers can go in cold. They find information. They retrieve data. They cannot retrieve memories like I can. They've never Extracted a being from a layer of someone's memory before. So their Preceptors dispatch them like officers on a raid. They go in, gather information, and get out.

Maybe that's why I prefer undercover cop movies and detective shows to military or police-force action movies. I like the strategic plotting, the secret lives, the blurring of lines. The blurring of business and personal lines is tricky for me, though. How can I not become invested in my beings?

Tobias says it will get easier for me to detach from my mission once it's over. But right now I still think about what happened to that little girl and get goose bumps. I still worry about the brother. He is still alive, isn't he? Did I do enough? Is my orphan strong enough to go through this world alone? And my last girl. My age. Beautiful. Graceful. Sweet. So sensitive. So twisted. Her mother should have stopped pushing her, should have stopped criticizing her after my Extraction. Did I do enough to get her to stop torturing herself? Enough to get her to stop punishing herself?

Tobias has heard tell of only one other Seer like me, or actually, only one other Extractor, as I am called. I guess that's why I am paired with him; he's the only one who seems to have answers for me. Other Seers avoid me or look at me like they are either in awe of me or hate me because I make their awesome abilities seem second-rate. If I try to ask other Preceptors even the simplest of questions, it's always the same reply, "Ask Tobias."

On my first meeting for this mission, I learned the background on Miss Eri Kuono. Eri Kuono is the daughter of Marjorie and Arashi Kuono. Marjorie met Arashi while spending a year in Japan as a part of a Global Links learning abroad program. She was furthering her cultural studies as she worked toward becoming a translator and linguist. Arashi was completing his degree in neuroscience. When the year was up, they returned to the United States together. They married shortly after, pursued their careers, and had Eri four years into their marriage.

Marjorie has enjoyed unparalleled success in her field. Arashi's breakthroughs in neuroscience have been praised and acclaimed. Eri is bright, no doubt. Alsinboro Academy bright. You can't be a slouch in the intellect department and be accepted there. But she is not achieving to the level that is expected of her. Apparently this is a source of dissension in the house. Arashi is distracted. He has pulled back from his latest project to focus more direct attention on the potential successes of his only child.

Hence the mission. Tobias was contacted. Apparently the Seers are awaiting Dr. Kuono's newest breakthrough in neuroscience. I am to win Eri's confidence, uncover what lies at the center of her "lack of drive and inability to work to her known potential," and then Navigate Dr. Kuono. It is believed that the key to her discontent lies in his overbearing nature. If I can Extract a memory from Dr. Kuono, one that is at the center of his need for Eri to be as successful as he and his wife are, he may be able to accept her as she is, relax about what she will accomplish in the future, and get his focus back on work.

In today's meeting I report on the status of my relationship with Eri. In other words I recount our lone conversation. Tobias is pleased with the contact but stresses the need to form a deeper connection while I am still "the new girl." Being new carries an obvious appeal. My classmates will feel me out and see what group I settle down with. And then they will label me and feel that all is right with the world. School is like the post office that way. All mail sorted according to zip code. All packages weighed and stacked in piles, piles that will never again be together in one great mass as they were when they came in. We might all start as a batch of blubbering kindergartners and go out attached to a year as one graduating class, but all the time in between is spent in sliced-off divisions of sameness. Skaters together? Check. Future starving artists together? Check. The beautiful popular crowd in the VIP section? Check. And no matter my tastes or comfort zone, my group is a clear choice. Eri's group.

Tobias provides me more background information on Eri's group.

"They are the overachievers," he starts. "Luke Brewer is her main companion. I originally believed them to be a couple, but it seems they are platonic. Luke is a newer student to Alsinboro

Academy. He transferred in last year after two years at a private academy for boys in Boston. Daisy Underwood is the daughter of the most affluent family in Preston. Her parents are both surgeons and work at the Hospital of the University of Pennsylvania, here in the city. Eri's parents seem to tolerate the presence of Luke but foster her friendship with Daisy. Whom she spends her time with seems of particular interest to them."

Great. So I may have to sell myself to her parents if I want to spend any real time with her. It's fortunate for me that Tobias leaves no loose ends when preparing my background information and credentials. At least I know her parents will find my pedigree acceptable.

Supposedly I spent my freshman year abroad, studying in England at a Cambridge preparatory school for young writers. I spent my sophomore and junior years in New Hampshire with an aunt, splitting my time between tutors and taking classes at an all-girls institution that primes young ladies for Ivy League educations and careers that will ensure there is no shortage of women in leadership and power-heavy roles in business.

In reality I have spent the last year traveling into brains and taking memories from them. I have been living in a two-room apartment above the building Tobias owns, which is also a location headquarters for Seers. Before that? I have no idea. Would that be acceptable to Dr. and Mrs. Kuono? A girl with a strange ability to raid brains but with no power over the memories in her own? I'm going to have to trick myself into believing that I can hang with their crowd, that I belong in their elite world of success and riches. The only thing I know I can match is their intellect. I'll just have to focus on that in order to drum up my confidence.

"There's also Patrick Crown. Track star and crew captain. And Frances Nelson. She holds the record for youngest female to have achieved a perfect score on the SATs and will surely be the academy's valedictorian."

Uh, okay. Maybe *match their intellect* was a bit assuming. I'll just try to keep up.

"Be sure to secure an invitation into her home before next week," he says as he swivels his chair back to his four computers and data table. I am being dismissed.

Sure, Tobias. Piece of cake.

Chapter

The next morning I make my commute in twenty-six minutes. No traffic over the bridge, a speedy trip down 295 South. I pull into the parking lot a little early. There are cars scattered here and there, a Beamer, a bunch of Mercedes, a few domestic cars. And then my fire-engine red Dodge Dakota SLT Crew Cab. It stands out like a boiled lobster on a bed of rice. I will make no apologies for my truck, though. I love that truck. With my fire-licked hair, I never blend in anyway.

I walk the winding brick path to the academy doors. I take it all in. The beauty of this place. It's a brownstone that looks more like a church or a palace than a school. It has a slate roof with peaks and turrets. It's the most romantic building I have ever been expected to enter. The front doors are intricately carved walnut, curved, with brass hardware and lion's head knockers. I pull the right door toward me and enter the grand hall. Glass cases and gold-framed pictures of the academy founders greet me.

I do feel good here. In spite of myself I allow the grandness to reel me in. I want to belong here. If I knew myself, where I came from, would I be worthy of this place? Would I fit in here if Tobias hadn't created my résumé to fit the requirements?

I don't have time for self-discovery. I have to find Eri. And now that I know Eri's group, I will have to decide what to do about Ryan. I knew I needed someone the first week. I needed to get around the school, and I needed to not be seen as antisocial or a loner. He initiated our acquaintance, and he was a welcome friend. But now that I know the small circle that Eri surrounds herself with, I may have to drop him. Circles are fickle like that. You can join one if you're new, but you can't bring in an "old" student with you. Maybe if he's a floater—someone who transcends groups because of his usefulness or many activities or school political involvement—he can come with me. I kind of hope he can. I like him. And he's so freaking smart.

"Morning, Leesie."

I was expecting Ryan. I was not expecting him.

"I'm Luke. Luke Brewer." He smiles. I had seen pictures in the files Tobias provided and had seen him in the hallway, but the images and faraway glimpses had done him no justice. This boy is attractive. Fan-yourself attractive.

"I know. I mean . . . hi. Um, morning," I say as I shift my books and send one over the top and onto the floor.

Smooth, Leesie. Great work.

"Right." He seems amused by my fumble. He's still smirking when he rights himself after retrieving my fallen book. "Yeah, I guess you're getting to know some names around here. Listen, I was just going to invite you to sit with us at lunch today. Eri has told us a little about you, so I figured we all might as well know a little about you. Bring Ryan. He's welcome." He broadens his smile. God, his eyes are dark.

"Great. Sounds like a plan. I'll see you then." I continue down the hallway, leaving him there. I like to exit first. End the conversation first. Leave them wanting more, maybe. Never leave a guy wishing I'd just shut up already. I wasn't doing too well in the conversation department just now anyway. I have until lunch to get it together. I am supposed to come off as calm, collected, confident, *intriguing*.

Well, one question is answered and can be off my mind: I guess Ryan is a floater. He's welcome at their lunch table. Good. Great. This is perfect. Then why does it feel so weird? Why don't I feel good about the way things are working out? Because it's too perfect. Too easy. Why is Luke approaching me when my only contact has been with Eri? Shouldn't Eri have done the inviting? And why does he need to know what Eri knows? What does he want with me?

I go through my morning distracted and anxious. I see them all in the hallway at various times. Senior wing is a horseshoe of three hallways, so running into them is inevitable. Daisy and Eri glance at me and offer polite half smiles. They show cautious interest, but not over-excitement. Frances seems to see no one but her instructors. Her focus is amazing. She has almost no interaction with her peers in the hallway. It's like an expert dancer coming on the dance floor during a song. The amateurs part and watch her work. Seeing Patrick is like seeing someone famous. Patrick sees all and is sure that all see him. He is Mr. Hollywood. When he sees me, he gives me a broad, dentist's dream of a smile. If the Ken doll where a real boy, his name would be Patrick Crown.

The members of Eri's group all seem to fit easily into a category. It's only Luke's category that bothers me. I see Daisy and Patrick talk to Luke between classes. He listens, glances their way, nods, but I only see him actually *speak* to Eri. He watches her so protectively. Like a guardian. Like a boyfriend. Tobias said they were not together, but it's hard to tell that by watching him watch her. Only he's not just watching her. He's watching me, too.

When I catch him, he makes no attempt to cover it up. He doesn't look away quickly or offer a smile. He simply continues to *watch* me. It's not staring. He's not looking me up and down or checking me out. He's watching my moves, my face, my eyes. Last week I saw only the back of him in the hallway and once at the drinking fountain. Today I see him at every turn. He always seems to know exactly where I am.

I know where to look when I enter the dining hall. They sit at a table in the center of the room. I had been sitting to their right with Ryan and a few others. Ryan hadn't seemed to react when I asked him to join me at Eri and her friends' table for lunch. He politely declined, saying he liked where he was. And there he was in his usual seat. I don't seem to be missed. I guess he was just the welcoming committee, and, with the invite for me to join a group removing my "displaced new girl" label, his job is done.

Patrick flashes me another award-winning grin and waves me over.

As I walk toward them, I take them all in. Patrick is flawless. He's muscled without being too bulky, has elegant features without appearing too polished, his blond hair is tousled and sun-streaked, and he's funny and easy-going. He would make it hard for me to be a boy in this school. Too fierce a competition. Eri's the smallest. Very petite. But her olive complexion, dark, shiny hair, and interesting features ensure that she's not overlooked. Daisy is cute. She's a dark blonde with light-green eyes. She's tan, though still paler than Eri. She's tall and athletically built. She's curvy but looks strong. She is the all-around teenage girl. Money, looks, great personality, and she actually seems like a decent person. And why wouldn't she be? She's got everybody beat anyway. Frances reminds me of Velma from *Scooby-Doo*. Not physically, but because of the seriousness she brings to the group. Could you imagine Scooby-Doo without Velma? All you'd have is the antics of Scooby, the voracious hunger and fumbling of Shaggy, the dumb-jockness of Fred, and the who-cares-about-the-brains-when-there's-a-short-dress-and-a-shock-of-hot-red-hair? of Daphne. Velma gives validity to the group, enough for them to call themselves mystery solvers. This good-looking group is smart on its own, but with Frances, it is a coveted group for its brains, *despite* its looks. I rest my eyes on Luke, last but not least.

I am inches from the table now. His body and chin are straight, facing Patrick, who sits opposite him, but his eyes are focused to his left. On me. My lips part as I inhale at . . . at what? Being caught checking all of them out? Analyzing them? Or at his face? That perfect face.

"Hey, Leesie! Welcome! I'm Patrick. You've met Eri and Luke. This is Frances, and this is Daisy." He gestures to each of his friends as he goes around the table. "So, Eri says you seem okay. We figured we'd find out for ourselves. How do you like it here so far?"

I snap out of it and focus on the task at hand, which I'm sure will be a series of questions. The first of which is a trick question. *How do I like it here so far?* I have to be positive or else I am a whiner. But if I'm too positive, I defy the laws of normal teenage angst. "It's an adjustment, but I like it okay."

I answer some more expected questions: *What was your old school like? Why did you transfer?* I answer according to my created backstory.

"I lived with my aunt in New Hampshire before I moved here. She had me set up with tutors, and I took classes at a school nearby. It was a nice place, lots of land. She ran a stable, so there was always something to do. I loved spending time with the horses."

"Ooh, do you ride?" Daisy asks. "You'll have to come riding with me if you do. I have two horses boarded nearby."

"I did ride. And thanks. I'd love to get back on a horse." That part's true. I see images of horses in the foggy mess of a memory I have.

"Let her continue, Daisy," Luke says, bringing us back to what I guess is important to him: my bio.

"About a year ago my aunt got sick. Cancer. When she found out, she began to make arrangements for me to attend Alsinboro. She had talked before about it being the best on the East Coast. My education, even to her death, was her top priority."

"So, she . . . " Frances hesitates.

"Yes. She died two months ago." I drop my eyes instinctively. Even if I didn't really lose "my aunt," I've lost everyone I knew. Considering I have no past, no clear non-Seer memories, and no family, this fake loss pales in comparison to my real one. So I really don't feel like watching them pity me.

"We're so sorry, Leesie," Patrick offers.

"Thank you." I glance around the table at the concerned faces, hoping they feel as if they have looked appropriately concerned long enough and are ready to go back to being just plain curious. I stop at Luke's. He's frowning.

"So who do you live with now?" His voice borders the line of casual interview and inquisition.

"I live with my legal guardian, I guess until my eighteenth birthday." Mostly true. I live above him. Alone.

"Legal guardian? You have no parents?" Eri, who had until now remained silent, is wide-eyed and somewhere between shock and awe. I can understand her reaction, knowing what I do about her. She swims in the middle of the pool—at the shallow end is the safety net of her family's love, and in the deep end is the imminent drowning she feels as they weigh their expectations on her shoulders.

"Nope. No parents." We lock eyes. She purses her lips, turns the corners down, and nods slightly as if to say, *Well, okay, then.* She says more in that nonverbal gesture than she could have aloud. She says she doesn't know what to say, so she isn't going to try. I like that. Besides, she doesn't need to say anything. What is there to say?

Around the table there is a tag team exhale as we all take a break from my heavy sharing. Daisy is the first to attempt to lighten the mood. "Hey, we're all going to watch Patrick and his crew team annihilate the competition this afternoon. Want to come along?"

"Sure. Sounds like fun. You're all going?"

"We're *all* going," Luke says with emphasis. I still can't tell if he is interested in me because he is simply selective about who can join the group or because he wants to make sure I *don't* join the group. I hate to break it to him, though: no matter how he feels about it . . . I'm in.

Chapter

I have studio art with Eri after lunch, but we don't walk there together. Luke hustles immediately after Eri and sets their quick pace. I'm behind, with Daisy and Patrick. Frances is already back in work mode and has moved off on her own. Daisy and Patrick chat about the arrangements for the afternoon. They'll take two cars. Eri will drive Daisy and Luke in her car, and Frances and I will ride with Patrick in his. Someone will drop me off at my truck afterward. Obviously my goal is to be as close to Eri as I can get, but, because I cannot be obvious, I can't attempt to change the car situation. Besides, getting close to her friends is a step closer to her at this point.

There's more to it than that, though. I want to get close to her for the success of my mission, of course. I am committed to my mission and to achieving my goal for myself and for Tobias. But what is it? Why does it already feel like more? I get attached to my mission subjects. Tobias is working with me on that. But it usually happens later as a result of spending so much time invested in someone's life. Why, then, do I feel such a strong connection to her now? Not an attachment. A connection. Why does this mission already feel so different? As I weave through the halls, I make a mental note to address this creeping connection with Tobias, though I can imagine the lecture that will follow.

Eri and I have eased into a comfortable arrangement in art. We usually chat for the first fifteen minutes of the period while we set up, and then we settle down to work. We comment on each other's progress and artistic genius halfway through, and with ten minutes remaining, we help each other clean up. We've become easy partners. The conversations aren't forced, and the silences aren't awkward. It's become my favorite part of the day, which used to be my lone commutes here and back in my truck.

However, when I walk into art today, Eri is already getting to work.

"Hey." I put my books down and look over at her, smiling, expecting to see her smiling back at me. Instead her eyes are on her painting. She's even frowning as if to ensure that she looks super into it, a true frustrated artist. There's only one problem. She just got here. She and Luke were pretty fast in the hallway, but what, did they strap on jetpacks and sail down here? She just slapped that painting down a second ago—I know it. Why is she trying to appear so busy?

"Hey," she answers. She doesn't look up. She doesn't smile. "I'm so behind on this."

There she goes, frowning again. Come on, Eri. No Oscar for this performance. You don't want to talk to me. I get it. But why?

Lunch went well, I thought. Her friends seemed to like me. All except Luke. Could he have said something to her? Could he have decided that what he found out about me doesn't work for him or the group? That's got to be it. He doesn't approve of me.

Just as quickly as I blame Luke for Eri's silent treatment, I decide how to handle it. Do nothing. It's not my style to do the whole "Are you mad at me?" thing. Too girly and childish. I also don't force myself on anyone. I always take the hint.

"Sure. I have a lot of work to do, too."

And I do. I get right to work. As I sit there, though, I question if this reaction, just letting her be, is the right one. Sure, it's what comes naturally to me. I am not a chaser. I like to be chased. Hunted. Wanted. I am most comfortable when it's others doing the asking. It's not that I don't like to be around people. I do. But I also don't mind being alone. And the idea of being with someone who doesn't want to be with me, just the idea of it, makes me squirm.

I saw a movie a few weeks ago. The movie was about a young girl and her first crush. What sticks with me is not the girl's character or her crush's. It was the girl's older brother. He was the most popular boy in school, a lady's man, and, of course, as predictable movies go, a huge jerk to the girl. One of the things he would do is make her into his secretary. He was juggling so many girls at once that he needed his sister to take messages for him and make excuses as to why he was unavailable—meaning out with another girl or simply avoiding her. The phone rang constantly. Girl after girl called and called again.

"Tell Janie I'm at work. Tell Samantha I'm playing basketball. Tell Michelle I'm busy. Tell Rachel I died. . . ."

Blatant lies, eyes rolling when he was told what girl was on the phone, constant complaining about the ones who just wouldn't take a hint.

And that was all it took for me. Now I imagine a boy on the phone with his friend after a date with me telling the friend that he would rather have been out with anyone else but me and wishing I had never asked him out in the first place. It has become my greatest fear. I have no friends, no family, no real relationships, so when I meet potential candidates for the job openings, I need to be sure they want to be in my life for good. Missions allow reprieve from my fears, considering these are not meant to be genuine social interactions that star me as myself. Even so, I know that I can never truly separate my natural social instincts and my mission character. But I will take measures whenever I can to ensure that when I am around someone, he or she wants me there. I figure if I get someone else to do the asking, for my name, for my number, for my friendship, for my time, he or she must want to be around me.

Eri and I are different. This relationship cannot be optional, and I can't take the hint or refuse to reach out to my mission subject. She's the whole reason I'm here. If she gives me the brush-off permanently, my mission is over. And what do I tell Tobias? *Oh, I'm sorry to disappoint you and every other Seer in existence, but my mission subject doesn't like me anymore, and, see, I have this thing about forcing myself on people. . . . I need her to reach out to me.* Yeah, that'll go over well.

Okay. I'll wait until ten minutes to the end of the period. I'll leave my comfort zone. I'll initiate. I can do this.

With fifteen minutes left in the period, I can't take it any longer. The flip-flopping in my stomach has become annoying and if I don't start this soon, I'll be so annoyed and amped up

I'll probably start with her instead of reaching out to her.

"Did you get a lot done? How's it coming along?" Good. A yes-no question and then one that requires elaboration. She'll have to talk enough that I can feel out her body language and tone.

"Yeah, I guess. It's looking okay." She keeps her eyes down and to the left. She is wagging her crossed leg. Her shoulders are slumped forward. Her dark straight hair covers all but the outer inch of them. She's pinching her full lips together slightly. Her voice is quiet, a little squeaky and unsure. She's . . . wait a minute. . . . She's not mad. She's not avoiding me maliciously. The pose, the voice, like a chastised child. She's guilty? She's feeling guilty? For what?

"Are *you* okay?" Here I go, diving in the Sea of Put Yourself Out There.

"I guess . . . I . . . I just feel so bad!" She blurts out the last part as if it had been burning her tongue for quite some time.

"Bad for what? What did you do? You didn't do anything." I'm talking too fast, but I'm afraid she'll shut down again.

"About your parents. About you having no parents." Eri looks up at me now. Her eyes are pleading. She is genuinely upset! What is with this girl? I play back the scene at the lunch table in my head. She seemed shocked to find out, but she didn't do or say anything wrong that I could remember. She didn't do anything to feel bad about. Did she?

"Eri, thanks, but you don't have to feel bad for me. I'm okay. I—"

Eri shakes her head and interrupts, "Leesie, do you know

what I was thinking when I heard you say that? Do you know the first thing that came to my mind when I found out?" She jerks her head up and looks me straight in the eyes. She pauses. And the quiet, squeaky, unsure tone of her voice is replaced by a matter-of-fact evenly stated "I was jealous."

Uh, okay?

She's still looking at me. She's waiting for me to say something. She wants my gut reaction. I decide to minimize the situation.

"Jealous? Yeah, I get it." She doesn't seem satisfied, so I continue, "I know how parents can be even if I don't have any. And I know how it is to look at someone else's situation and, problems and all, wish you had it instead of your own. I get it, Eri."

"I just feel like an ingrate. To acknowledge in my head, and now to you, that I would rather be an orphan than have my parents. I'm sorry. I shouldn't have told you. I don't know why I did."

We lock eyes again. I notice for the first time the yellow flecks in her brown eyes. I really look at her. She has a round face with high cheekbones and a strong jaw. She has Asian features from her dad. Her eyes are almond shaped, big, but lighter brown than if she were all Japanese. Her mom must have light eyes, hazel maybe. Eri is clearly beautiful.

But she doesn't radiate beauty; she radiates mediocrity, if that's possible. If she were a campfire, she would be the fire you awake to in the middle of the night. Not the roaring flames you went to bed to, told stories around, roasted marshmallows in. The one that burns highest and brightest. And not the fire everyone will wake to in the morning, only glowing embers left, smoking and snuffing themselves out. The one with nothing left to offer. No, she'd be the calm, low fire that burns when no one is watching. The one that keeps everyone warm but gets no rubbing hands held over it, no admiring faces, no *oohs* and *ahhs* as it pops and crackles. She's the fire whose only purpose is to be a fire and stay lit through the night. And my job is to find out why that is.

"I'm glad you told me" is all I say. I haven't felt the need to overstate anything with her. I don't feel like I have to say too much or fully explain myself.

"Me, too," Eri says slowly, as she gathers her books. "I guess I'll see you at Patrick's meet."

"Yep. See you."

I walk the halls now like Frances, staring straight ahead and seeing no one. My head is so full. First the anxiety before the lunch meeting. Then the question-and-answer session at lunch. And then Eri's jealousy. I can't wait to get home to sort through all this in my head. I need to be alone to think. But that isn't going to be possible for a while. So I better get into a social mood, or at least pretend, because it's almost time for group meeting number two.

Chapter

We meet in the parking lot after school. It turns out that Patrick Crown's race is in Philly, so the driving arrangements we made before no longer make sense. We decide that Eri will still drive Daisy and Luke in her car, Patrick will take Frances, and I'll be driving alone.

"This way you can head right home after the meet," Patrick says.

"Yeah, sure. No problem. I can meet you guys there," I answer, masking my displacement. I wanted to be alone with my thoughts, but not between gatherings. I begin to fear my ability to bounce back into conversation mode after being quiet and in my head during the drive. Plus this driving arrangement makes me feel out of the circle when I'd been so sure they were inviting me in. I've gone from being one of them to being someone just showing up to watch the Mighty Patrick row his way to stardom.

I wait with Frances while Patrick gathers and loads his gear into his car. He is two meets away from earning a spot on the national rowing team. Today's meet could inch him to the next level.

The race is at Boathouse Row. I don't know much about the area except that there is money there. A lot of money. I could tell that just from my view from I-95. Not that my area of the city is bad. There's nothing wrong with the Northern Liberties section of Philly, but it isn't the old money that Boathouse Row represents. These missions are funny like that. I have to get into circles of people no matter where they come from or what they have. And they have to be okay with me as I am. Regular. I'm sure I don't appear poor, but I know my companions are aware that I am no heiress. Or am I? Funny thing is, I have no idea. Do I come from money? Were my parents scraping by, middle class, destitute? Tobias pays my expenses now. He pays for my food, clothing, my phone. I guess you could say I "work" for him and the Seers organization. I have no identity where money is concerned. I think that frees me in a way, I decide. I get to base my worth and how I am perceived by others on something other than class and status.

"So, Frances, what's this going to be like?"

"You've never been to a crew meet before?" I shake my head, and she continues: "Well, we'll see the start and the end. His crew will break away from the pack pretty early, and they'll round a bend. Then we wait. His team will be the first one we see heading back. We cheer. He smiles. The end."

She's matter-of-fact, not condescending or annoyed. She seems almost pleased with being able to describe future events with so much assurance as to how they will turn out. She seems to like bragging about her friend.

"Okay. Good. I like to know I am the guest of the one who will be in the winner's circle."

"Ready, guys?" Patrick slams the trunk of his Mercedes. "I want to be a little early. Leesie, I won't see too much traffic, will

I? My races aren't usually right after school like this."

"We should be good. I haven't been having a hard time getting home."

"Great."

Patrick looks away from me to address the rest of the group, "Give Leesie your phone numbers in case we get separated. Parking can be tight. I'll text the dock's address. Everybody follow me!"

Patrick gives a wave to Eri, Luke, and Daisy to get them in motion. They're on the other side of the parking lot and seem to have been watching us. They wave back and pile into Eri's car.

I'm relieved that Patrick didn't ask me to lead. I'm sure he's had meets at Boathouse Row before and is comfortable driving there. But I've noticed South Jersey people tend to make the Philly people do the piloting. Too many one-way streets and two-way stops. This way I get to blindly follow.

I settle into driving, paying attention to the types of cars on the road, to how many red lights we hit before getting on the highway, to the tractor-trailer driver who slows to let us all merge over to take the Ben Franklin Bridge exit, to the lady in the toll booth whose hair is dyed the color of a maraschino cherry, to the way Eri hugs the wall in the right lane of the bridge. Most people hug the center line, almost crossing it, afraid their car will sideswipe the wall, the only barrier between car and river. Having a wall on one side makes most people feel penned in and vulnerable. But I hug the wall, too. I like having something solid next to me the way I like to lean against the solid steel of an elevator as I move up or down at speeds I don't care to know. I also like the inside seat at a booth or a captain's chair over one with no arms. A more controlled environment.

When we park at Boathouse Row, I'm overwhelmed by how lovely it is. The boathouses, with their sharp-peaked roofs and colorful beams over white or tan stucco, are a perfect contrast against the Schuylkill River. Some are Tudors, some grand stone structures with turrets and columns. One house has a red top half that highlights three half-oval windows. The bottom portion of the house is a cream color. The bright-red door with white trim around the window is like sparkling teeth in a smiling ruby-lipped mouth. The effect is something out of a fairy tale. Surely this is the house Hansel and Gretel couldn't resist entering. The bustle of the city shakes hands with the calm of the water, and I am better. I suddenly feel like I could stay here all day. I don't want the afternoon to end.

I shake myself from my architectural daze to the issue at hand. This afternoon will end, but not before I become comfortable in this group. I have to meld into them seamlessly, an easy fit. And that is not going to happen if I keep gawking at boathouses instead of getting out of the truck and joining them.

Watching Patrick ready for the race is like watching a marble wind through a perfectly constructed Mouse Trap game. He moves through the steps of getting his equipment set up to entering the water as if it is all one extended action. I don't know much about boating or crew teams or a bunch of beautifully muscled boys rowing in perfect sync with one another, but I know that Patrick makes it look simple and graceful. I, as well as every female nearby age nine to ninety-nine, have my eyes fixed on him. He gives a final wave to his entourage just before the race begins and he is off. There is no talking, only oohs and ahhs as the teams traverse the water and a pace is set. Once Patrick's team has a substantial lead and has rounded the bend, the crowds disperse a little and conversations resume.

"What do you think so far?" Daisy asks me.

"It's incredible. An experience. Just seeing Boathouse Row from this angle is new for me. And you're right, Patrick is amazing. Thanks for inviting me along today." I'm sure to look at each of their faces to show that the sentiment is meant for the group and not just for Daisy.

"Happy to have you here," Luke responds quickly and sounds cordial except for the way he held on to the "here" longer than he should have. It sounded clenched and forced. Am I just reading too much into everything he does now? Or does he really have something against me?

"Thanks, Luke." I say his name on purpose. I've noticed if people don't like someone or have a conflict with someone, being addressed by name by the person can ignite something. I am looking for any sign at this point. And I get it.

As soon as I utter his name, he jerks his head to face me. He lifts his chin slightly in defiance. He puffs his chest. His eyes, his coal-black eyes, pierce mine. But then he half smiles and nods once. But it comes too late. He recovers too late. I have my answer. He has a problem with me. But what? And why? And, most important, how is this going to complicate my getting close to Eri if he is her obsessed platonic-yet-boyfriendy bodyguard?

Conversation continues but is centered on Patrick and when he is going to come back around toward the end of the race. Finally we see him. His team is out in front by two hundred yards at least. His team strokes the way a millipede simultaneously moves its legs. The boys glisten in the sun, and the water glints off their oars. They make such a beautiful spectacle that once again my surroundings distract me.

"Quite a sight, isn't it?" Eri has moved beside me as the crowd shifts to watch the end of the race.

"They don't look real." I glance over as I say this and am surprised to see that she is looking directly at me.

"Real. Humph. Privileged, smart, athletic young men in water sports. They aren't real." She keeps throwing me these loaded statements. She wants to tell me something. I can feel it. And then there's Luke. There is so much going unsaid right now. I have to take a deep breath. Maybe a few. It's usually about this time that I go into somebody's brain just to do something to someone.

"They won! They won! Oh, Patrick! Oh, honey!"

Frances identifies the screaming woman as Patrick's grandmother, and I watch as Patrick is surrounded in seconds, and our group is kicked back a few feet as family members take their places closest to Patrick. Frances says at most meets it can take fifteen minutes or more for them to get their chance to congratulate him.

The sun is low in the sky before the group is loading up to return to Preston. No one says the obvious to me, and that is, "You can leave any time, Leesie. You're not coming back with us." No one seems in a hurry despite the fact that it's going on seven o'clock, we haven't eaten, and we all have a ton of homework to do. I decide to initiate my exit before they do. *Leave while the party is still good and don't overstay your welcome.*

"I'm gonna head home, guys. Thanks for the invite today. It was a lot of fun. Congrats again, Patrick."

"You're leaving?" The urgency in Eri's voice takes me by surprise. It must have taken Luke and Daisy by surprise as well because they look over at her with raised eyebrows and silent concern.

"Uh, yeah. I was going to. I mean, I'm starving and I have a lot to do before tomorrow." I make sure I say "was going to" and throw in an "I'm starving."

"I'm hungry, too. Maybe you could show us a place around here to eat? Or a place by you?" She hangs on to the second question. She wants to go by my place. Check out where I live. Maybe she's just curious about what it's like to live in the city. Maybe she's still on this "How does a kid with no parents live?" kick. Maybe she's seeing if I check out. Suddenly I feel like I am the one being Navigated. Who's the center of a mission here, Eri or me?

"Sure. There's a diner by me. Only about ten minutes west of here. Who wants to go?" I look at their faces, hoping to be able to tell if they all really want to go or if they'll feel obligated to say yes because Eri initiated the whole thing.

"I'm too hungry to make it home. We'll all go, right?" Patrick answers with a smile so wide with victory that no one would dare refuse him. In fact, no one really bothers answering. They just turn and head to the cars in obedience. I wonder if that's what it's always like with them, if they always follow one another like a school of fish or a flock of geese. Normally I would be put off by the idea of sameness and of going along with the crowd, but with these guys it feels fair, unforced, and like they're being together trumps the importance of being in charge.

"So, where're we going?" Eri is beside me. She falls into step with me easily.

"A place called Tuie's. It's pretty good."

"Great. We'll follow you." She glances back at Luke before she says this. She drops her voice at the "you." She smiles with the left side of her mouth. The right side is up slightly in a smirk. I haven't seen this look on her face before. It's not shy, nervous, slightly insecure, and sweet. It's something much more determined, purposeful.

As we all get back in our cars, I can't help but wonder . . . I came here alone, following them. I leave here alone but as the leader, taking them closer than anyone has been to where I live. How did this juxtaposition happen? I keep giving information, letting them in. Aren't I the one who is supposed to be getting the information? I should be following them around Preston right now. I should be going to *their* favorite diner or to one of *their* houses. I should be sitting in Eri's room getting her to divulge all her secrets to me. Why does she seem to manipulate things to make me the center instead of her? And why is Luke always there to back her up or to listen in? And when I meet again with Tobias, what am I going to report? That I am a pawn in Eri's chess game? That I am being played? Am I? Is she onto me? No. How could she be? But why does it feel like she has her own agenda?

Chapter

As we head west on Girard Avenue toward the diner, I am crawling in my own skin. Here I am in my neighborhood—at the center of my mission—with a bunch of highly intelligent and intuitive kids whose idea it was to come around here. I'm beginning to panic. It's the kind of panic I imagine a kid feels as he sneaks out of his parents' house to go to a party in the next neighborhood over. As he leaves his house and walks down his own street, he likely ducks his head, trying to make himself invisible. Suddenly every car is his neighbor's car. Every guy walking his dog is the guy who's friends with his dad. Every face he passes could be the person who says, "Hey, I saw your son out walking last night. Everything okay?" It's only when he enters into the next neighborhood that a veil of anonymity makes him feel safe, like he might actually pull this off. I feel this, only I am heading out of anonymity and into familiarity.

I am scanning the streets for the regulars I see all the time. There's the flowing skirt lady. She wears these long prairie skirts and rides her bike all over the place. I keep waiting for the skirt to tangle in her pedals and for her to do a flip over the handlebars into oncoming traffic. There's newspaper guy. He buys a paper at about seven or eight every evening and then sits out front of the fire station at Fourth and Girard and reads the paper in the waning sunlight. He's gonna drive himself to a state of blindness. There's chain-smoker girl. I don't actually know if she's a chain smoker, but whenever I see her, she's on the corner of Germantown Avenue lighting up another one. I've never spoken to these people. I've never stopped to chat or to introduce myself. I probably never will. And yet they, and a handful of others, have become my neighbors. They're my "borrow a cup of sugar/invite them in for tea" neighbors, if only in my head. I know I have no roots, but that doesn't stop my tree from dropping seeds. And now I feel like they may be watching me leading this caravan and waiting to question my intentions. Or the group's.

I pull into the lot on Germantown and wait for Patrick and Eri to park.

"That was easy to get to! What part of the city is this?" Patrick is wide-eyed and impressed.

"Northern Liberties."

"And you live here?"

"Nearby."

Oh, God, please don't ask to see my place. Hurry. Have an excuse ready.

"It's nice."

Good. Okay. Patrick has manners. He knows it's rude to invite yourself over to someone's house. He'll wait to see if he's asked, which will *not* happen. I just hope the others show the same restraint.

"The diner's this building here," I say, pointing across the street toward Second. The diner's back is to us, but we can see the wrought-iron tables to the side and the orange and teal décor through the floor-to-ceiling windows facing us. We form a lateral line and head toward it like a pack of wolves.

"You guys want to sit outside or in?" I ask trying to avoid the fumbling that will take place if I allow the host to ask that question once we're already inside.

"Let's sit outside. I want to see the neighborhood," Frances says. She's been quiet since the race. She probably wants to go home. I know she's got homework. We all do. At least that means they won't linger. They'll eat and go back to Jersey. And I'll be able to sort my brain out before I have to go back to them tomorrow and jumble it all back up.

The host with the big gauges, earrings that are more like space savers or hollow saucers creating a hole in each earlobe the size of a penny, and a merman tattoo on his forearm seats us facing the Piazza. It's the center part of the neighborhood, where most events take place. It's great for people watching. I come to the diner every couple days at least and sit by myself out here. I see it as part of my job. I have to be able to read people. I have to be able to make split-second decisions based on people's verbal, nonverbal, and facial cues. Plus it's fun. City people are especially fun to watch. They tend to use their bodies as extensions of their personalities more than suburbanites. There's hot-pink-hair guy, face-tattoo girl, and tons of people dressed so funkily that you know it has to be part of who they are and not just for attention.

It turns out the group enjoys people watching, too. That coupled with the fact that we have been together going on twelve hours has extinguished the need for constant conversation, thankfully. Even Eri lets up and concentrates on the short stack of pancakes she has ordered.

I fumble with my veggie wrap. I ordered the dressing on the side, but I can tell the cook forgot or missed the message, because the wrap is soggy and the sprouts are drenched. I'd send it back, but I don't want to mess up the relaxed feeling at the table. It's the second meal we've shared in one day. Because I spend so much time alone, the communal importance of eating with other people is not wasted on me, and I begin to feel, despite all the questions I have about Luke and Eri, like I am a part of this group. More than that. Like I *want* to be a part of this group.

I look from one member to the next. Frances and Daisy are talking and giggling. I follow their gaze and realize their eyes are following a guy wearing nothing but dangerously low-riding cut-off sweatpants. He is jogging through the Piazza as a glistening, muscle-bound thing of beauty. Wow. I tear my eyes away and look to the other end of the table. Patrick is making eyes at the cute blonde two tables away. Everywhere he's a star. Across from me Eri is treating butter and syrup as mediums in an art project as she readies herself to polish off the second half of her pancakes. Even Luke, sitting next to her, seems to have relaxed. The beef patty melt must be good. He is dipping fries into the juices left by the caramelized onions. He isn't watching me or frowning. And suddenly I am back to our first conversation in the hallway at school. The one where I couldn't speak calmly because his classic good looks threw me for a loop. All at once I am caught up in them again. His square jaw, his straight, thick eyebrows and a perfect hairline—the kind of hairline you know could never lead to baldness—his clear, clean skin, and nice lips—not too thick and not too thin.

"Leesie, you okay?"

I watch his lips form those words before I realize he is talking to me. And that he has obviously noticed me staring at him.

"Uh, yeah! Sure," I answer too quickly. What does it matter how well I cover it up? It's obvious to him that I was checking him out. What's funny is that for the first time since early this morning he seems amused and friendly instead of looming and accusatory. He is smirking at me. His coal-black eyes dance over my face. He likes it. Unnerving me. That much I know.

"Do I have something on my face?" he asks playfully, and his eyes lock mine. He peers into me and hangs onto each word. No attitude. No anger. Maybe just a little flirty. . . .

"No. Your face is fine." I meet his eyes. I hang on to my words. No attitude. No anger. Definitely flirty. *I'll play your game. I'll meet your bet and raise you.*

I don't know when the rest of the group stopped watching the Piazza and started watching us, but now I can feel Eri and Frances and Daisy and Patrick's eyes. They are looking from us back to one another and back to us. It's Eri who interrupts our staring match.

"Well, guys, I need a stretcher to wheel me outta here. These pancakes were crazy good but are sitting in my stomach like lead bricks. Shall we go?"

Daisy chirps, "Go? Sure, I'm ready. I think that hot jogger is waiting for me over there!"

She giggles and points toward the center of the Piazza. Tuie's outdoor seating, sectioned off with low wrought-iron fencing, offers a perfect view of the Piazza's best selling point, an open-area plaza with a projection screen that often shows old movies or Phillies games. The plaza is complete with an Astroturfed sunning area and more benches than I've ever seen filled.

"I love that setup. You ever hang out there, Leesie?" Frances asks as she takes in the scene.

"Yeah, Frans. She goes there all the time. In her string bikini. You don't have any tan lines, do you, Leesie?"

"You have problems, Pat," Eri chides, but she chuckles as she leans across the table to punch him in the arm.

"Can we check it out?" Daisy asks.

"He's gone, babe. The shape he was in? He's a 5K away by now," Patrick says, continuing to tease.

"Can we walk it? Just for a little while?"

This time it's Eri who asks. She looks from one member of the group to the other, but her eyes rest on Luke to answer.

"If it won't keep Frances from the time machine she's building in her basement, I guess we can stay a little longer," Luke jokes. A full stomach has relaxed him.

"I'm up for it. We're not keeping you, are we, Leesie?" Frances says.

Her words settle into me the way a mother bird settles into her nest. I am a fragile egg. I hope one day to know what the security of true friendship feels like. But under the downy warmth of her words, which tell me that she wants to be here, that her only worry is that *I* am not tiring of *them,* I am one step closer to being tough enough to crack my own shell.

I collect myself and look from one eager face to the next. All I can say is "Not at all. Let's go!"

In the plaza Patrick continues his teasing, Daisy and Frances continue their guy scouting, and Eri walks close to me with Luke on her other side. The conversation is easy, and we laugh often. As Patrick was the star of the afternoon, they allow me to shine in the evening as they ask questions about the shops and restaurants we pass.

Finally the conversation slows, and I catch Frances checking her phone for the time. Patrick is the one who initiates their exit.

"Thank you, guys, for being here for me today. Thanks, Leesie, for a great time. But school calls. Even the best of nights must end, I guess."

I walk them back to the free lot and give them directions to the highway. Despite the time and Patrick's reminder of school, no one seems in a real hurry to get on the road. Frances leans against my truck.

"I'm glad you came today," she says. "You made coming to the city more fun."

She has the cutest little face, which houses the smartest, sharpest eyes.

"I'm glad I came, too. I had to experience Patrick's wonderment for myself," I respond playfully. Patrick eats it up and gives me a light punch in the arm. Daisy laughs and pushes Patrick back in mock defense of me. Eri and Luke are watching with amused but serious looks on their faces. Eri reaches for the door handle.

"We really have to go," she says. "We all have things to do when we get home."

"Yes. And we all need to prepare for tomorrow," Luke adds.

No one questions his statement. Everyone just refocuses and begins to pile into their respective cars. No one wonders exactly what he means by what he said. Am I the only one?

He means homework, *right*? We need to prepare for tomorrow by doing our homework, *right*? Why does he have the power to make me feel like a ping-pong ball, so light and easy to send flying in one direction and another? I watch him watch me as he pulls away. Everyone else waves, smiles, beeps. He watches.

And apparently he prepares for the next day. *Okay. I guess I will, too.*

Chapter

As I unlock my front door, I can't believe how glad I am to be alone. I fumble around a little before my fingers find the switch and the front light goes on. The soft glow is enough to light almost the entire apartment, which is hardly a feat, considering how small it is. My apartment is above a storefront and warehouse Tobias owns. The deli occupies the front downstairs, and Tobias occupies the back. He transformed the warehouse into three small rooms: a workroom to house his computers and research equipment; a conference room where he meets with local and visiting Seers; and a third massive space I have never been in. Tobias presents information on a need-to-know basis, so I guess when I need to know, I'll be shown that room.

My apartment is nondescript in decorating style since I haven't decided what my style is. And since I don't have heirlooms or family photos, it's kind of plain, but I like it. Its grays and browns, hardwood and creams. Neutral and calm. And tonight? Quiet. And protecting me, allowing me to go into my own head and hit replay on a day full of sideways glances and loaded statements that I need to think through and figure out.

I close the door behind me, don't bother to turn any other lights on, and cross the living room to a club chair I set under the window in the eat-in area of the kitchen. It made more sense to have a comfy chair in this space than a dining table. Who's coming to dine with me? No one. So instead, I do my homework, eat, write in my journal, everything, in this chair under the window. If I could sleep in a curled position, I'd never leave it.

I plop down, ease my feet out of my shoes, and pull my knees to my chest. As I gaze out the window at the city lights and at the way the skyline attacks the blackened canvas dwarfing the stars, I think about the power it takes to illuminate the city. And then I think about my kind of power. Power of the mind. I am good at overthinking. Analyzing. Knowing more about a person than he knows about himself. I use facial cues, hand gestures, sighs, the raising of a brow . . . anything. I am used to being ridiculously good at it. Better than regular people. Better than every other Seer.

I realized how good I am on my first mission for Tobias. The missing-girl mission.

When Tobias gave me the background information for the mission, he said that the aunt was guarded and that no other Seer had been able to penetrate a layer to gain access to the desired information: where the child was, why, and who was responsible.

When a being is guarded, it means that for some reason, he or she is able to keep a Seer out. This can be because the being has built a defense against being Navigated and that his or her brain can actually defend itself against a Seer. More often, though, the being is wounded. Mentally sick. Dark. Abused. Dangerous. This clouds and blends the layers, making it impossible for most Seers to decipher where they are and where the desired information is. The layers in this case are more like a maze. Instead of traveling down, Seers must twist and turn with confusing angles and sharp peaks. Most Seers cannot get in or cannot proceed. Tobias wanted to give me a try.

I had only been with Tobias a couple of weeks. Tobias said my first mission would be an easy one. One that would gauge my powers and rate me as a Seer. When I was prepped for the mission, though, it seemed anything but easy.

The little girl was seven. A red shock of curly hair blanketed her head and shoulders. Blue eyes. Freckles, of course. Chubby cheeks. A crooked, teeth-missing smile. Basically one of the cutest kid pictures I had ever seen. And she had been missing for six days. The family had reason to suspect that the child's aunt had something to do with the disappearance. Why? She was off. She would go away for a day. No one would know where she was. When the family questioned the aunt, she'd swear she had been home all day, cleaning. The worst of it was that the family didn't think the aunt was lying. They thought she had lapsed into another state of consciousness, that something had snapped. They feared she was bipolar or schizophrenic. They had been seeking help for her when the girl went missing. A cousin of the little girl was a Seer; he was the one who had attempted and failed the first Navigation, and he had contacted Tobias for help.

I started at the aunt's daughter's school. The aunt's daughter, Maggie, was, by strategy, in most of my classes. All I had to do was befriend her and gain access to her house to get to the aunt.

I watched Maggie that first day. She was a little shy. She played with her hair when she was unsure of herself or of what to say. She crossed and uncrossed her legs a lot. She wiggled her right foot from side to side when her right leg was crossed over her left, but when she switched legs and her left was crossed over her right, she didn't wiggle her left foot at all. She seemed to be more at ease when the left leg was crossed. When the right foot was wiggling, she seemed to be agitated or bored. When she was annoyed, she flared her nostrils. When she was concentrating, she furrowed her brow. So a furrowed brow for Maggie was okay; she was just interested. A furrowed brow with flared nostrils? Back off. She used her mouth to communicate nonverbally. She smirked a lot. She smirked when she found something amusing, but at someone else's expense. The teacher had accidentally gotten a pen mark on her own face at some point during class. Maggie smirked. So if I saw her smirking at me, I would be rushing to the nearest mirror. She bit her lower lip. This seemed to be when she looked at any boy she thought was cute. She pursed her lips. This mainly occurred when she was called on to answer a question or participate in class. So I guess she pursed whenever she felt pressured to speak. She sucked her teeth. She licked her top lip. I watched these cues. I memorized these cues. By the time we had our first conversation, she was comfortable around me at once because I knew when to engage.

"Hi. I'm Leesie. I'm new. Do you mind if I sit here?" I gestured to the seat next to hers. "I sat in the back yesterday and had a hard time seeing."

"Sure." Her right foot wiggled. "No one usually sits there."

Of course I knew that. The seat had remained empty the day before.

She uncrossed and recrossed with the left leg. Her foot was still.

"How do you like it here so far?" she asked. No flaring. She wasn't annoyed. No pursing. She wanted to speak. Good.

"I like it okay. Have you always gone here?"

A slight purse. Too loaded a question. I hadn't thought that through. What if she had moved a lot? Or wished she could get away?

"I guess I ask that question because I've moved around a lot myself," I added quickly.

"Oh. Right. That makes sense. Yeah, I've never moved before. I'm Maggie, by the way." She leaned toward me and began to fill me in on the teacher. Doesn't give too much homework, tests come directly from lectures and not from the textbook, so take good notes, etc.

Maggie had been a loner, which made sense, considering what she confided in me before she invited me over. It took a few weeks to secure an invite. Before I was to come for dinner, she warned me about her mother, telling me not to be surprised if she said or did something crazy. I reassured Maggie. I played the role of a wounded teen affected by the instability of constantly relocating. One wounded soul who understood another.

I remember sitting across from the aunt at the dinner table. Her light-brown eyes were shifty. Her body language was erratic. She was definitely guarded.

She looked up to ask me how I liked my new school. Everything about the woman shouted unpredictability. I couldn't risk her taking off. I focused on her left eye and went in.

Usually it feels like I am swimming through salt water. There's a thickness to the water but I can move freely through it. This felt colder than usual. And I'd say it was thicker than usual, but it varied. There was an inconsistency to her brain that was immediately alarming. I knew why the other Seer couldn't go in.

I sloshed back and forth and rolled in spirals as I attempted to travel down. Was this the way down? Where was I? Was that a layer over there? How had I ended up going sideways? I started looking for clues. In an unguarded brain the layers are defined by a gel-like ribbon. It reminds me of a finish line at the end of a race that you have to break through.

In a guarded brain it's not defined. The only thing I had to go on was the change in consistency in thickness and the temperature changes. I decided to go on temperature. I would follow the cold.

It was colder on my left side than my right, so I turned my head to the left and propelled myself in that direction. The cold enveloped me to my waist before what felt like ice chips began to sting my face. Was this another layer? I must be deeper down. Because the little girl had only been missing a few weeks, I didn't want to go deep. I just wanted to be in. I strained through murky grayish-brown to See the scene in front of me. The view was from a bridge. A low cement bridge. A neighborhood bridge. A small lake. A blue car. Parked just over the bridge at the water's edge. Two figures in the water. One tall. One small. And red-haired. A little girl flailing her arms at her sides, kicking her legs wildly. The girl was struggling to raise her head, a head that was being held down under the water by the taller, older figure. The aunt was drowning the girl.

I immediately went back to the fact that the aunt never remembered where she'd been after being gone all day. This memory existed, but for some reason, probably due to her mental illness, this layer was repressed. She was not hiding the truth. She didn't know the truth! She murdered her niece and didn't know when or why.

My eyes were kicking up to a full-on burn, so I needed to act. I reached out and down. I put one hand on the aunt and one on the drowning girl. I squeezed my frozen, clumsy fingers around the arm of the aunt and around the biggest chunk of the girl's red hair I could grasp and yanked them both up with me. I needed to pull this memory to the aunt's outermost layer. Into her most recent memories. If I could leave this memory with those, it would bring the scene to her current state of consciousness. The aunt would see what she had done.

With both hands full I had to feel for the warmth of the outer layer with my face and shoulders. I began to See scenes of what must have been today, going food shopping, making dinner. This was it. Her most recent memories. I let the aunt and the little girl go. I felt the top of the layer on my head and closed my eyes. I was out.

The room looked as if someone had put a pink lightbulb in the lamp. Pink was better than red, I remember thinking as I closed my eyes quickly, gently rubbed my eyelids, and swept pink tears off my cheeks. I knew that if my moving the memory had worked, there would be enough going on in the room within milliseconds that I couldn't afford to call attention to my almost bleeding eyes. I heard the aunt's shrieking before I could open my eyes again. I made my exit as Maggie picked up the phone to call the police. The aunt had thrown herself atop the dinner, which she sent crashing to the floor. She was striking herself and tearing out her hair in bloody chunks as she screamed over and over, "I killed her! I killed her! I killed Anna! God help me! I killed her!"

So in my first mission, I proved I could read people's cues and Navigate brains that most Seers cannot. I could move memories. I proved myself to Tobias, who said he hadn't expected so much of me so soon.

But I also saw a dead girl.

Remembering how supposedly talented I am does offer encouragement as I think about my current mission, but it certainly doesn't make me feel warm and fuzzy inside.

After journaling details from my current mission for Tobias, I put my pencil down and slide my journal under the cushion of my chair. I feel as if my brain itself is heavy and stuffed. I am almost relieved when a three-beat knock at the door pulls me from my unsorted thoughts. It's Daniel. He's a Preceptor who assists Tobias with his research. He is also the one sent to fetch me when Tobias wants to touch base. I retrieve my journal, slip on my shoes, and head for the door.

"Hello, Daniel," I say before the door is fully open.

"Elise. How are you this evening?"

"Okay."

"Tobias would like a word."

"Right."

I follow Daniel down the cold metal stairs and turn right at the landing. A long hallway dimly lit stretches out in front of me. Tobias's office door is within a few feet.

"Have a good night, Elise."

"You, too."

I turn the knob and slink inside. I walk briskly to the center of the room and take my seat in the padded chair in front of Tobias's desk. He has not swiveled around to address me yet, but my job is to hustle into my seat, set my journal in the center of his leather desk pad, and wait for his cue.

"Elise," Tobias starts mid-swivel, "was your day eventful?"

Tobias doesn't have an accent. He is American-born. He told me so. But he hangs onto the ends of words in a singsong un-American, un-Philly kind of way. It makes him sound equal parts regal and condescending. Maybe it's the power. Maybe it's his status in the organization. Something about him has always kept me at arm's length. He's not cold. Chilly, maybe.

"I did."

"Tell me about it."

I fill Tobias in as he reads through my journal. I leave out nothing. I provide details from scoring the invite to Patrick's race to dinner and our time after.

"An eventful day indeed. What do you have in place for tomorrow? Have you secured plans with Ms. Kuono?"

"Not yet."

"Then, no?"

"No."

"It seems that after being so readily included today, tomorrow ought to present you similar opportunities."

"Yes."

"And remember, Elise." Tobias hangs my name in the air until he can effectively look me over. I know he is checking for clues as to my mood, to see if I am nervous or agitated. He's the one who stresses that I must always look for similar cues in others. "This mission is of the utmost importance. Dr. Kuono's work is vital to the future of the organization."

"I understand."

His chair squeaks as he begins to turn away.

"Tobias?"

"Yes, Elise?"

"What kind of work is Dr. Kuono doing?"

"The kind of work that could answer many questions for us. Including questions about you."

Chapter

My alarm yells at me an hour and a half before I normally get up. I have to do the homework I ignored last night. I only half pay attention to the answers I put down. It's not that I don't care about the work, but I almost can't pay perfect attention to it. My brain absorbs information like a sponge. I retain everything I hear in the lectures but take notes to avoid drawing attention to myself. I do the work to prove that I deserve to be in a school as elitist as Alsinboro but wouldn't dare to strip Frances of her impending title as valedictorian. I like her, plus, after seeing her in action, I think she'd give me a run for my money.

I keep the radio blaring on the way to school. I change channels every time the music slows down or mellows out. Like if I drown out my ears, I'll keep myself from thinking or worrying *or preparing*. Wasn't I supposed to prepare for today? What does Luke have in store for me? There I go again. I turn the radio up even more.

Classes up to lunch go fine. Everyone stays focused, has to, in order to do well. There isn't a whole lot of socializing, even between classes. I wave to members of the group as I see them. They all wave back in nondescript ways, except for Frances, who doesn't even see me. But lunch is next.

I walk into the dining hall and head for the salad bar. I fill my tray with lentil salad, an apple, and plain Greek yogurt and head their way. They are just like they were yesterday. Frances, Patrick, and Daisy are chatting and smiling away. Eri is looking at me with an expression I can't classify. It's just as I thought. All except for Luke. He's smiling at me.

I am instantly filled with equal parts of dread and warmth as I feel flutters in my stomach. Oh, great. So I am intimidated by him *and* infatuated with him? *Awesome.*

"Hey, Diner Girl!" Patrick zings as he slaps the empty seat next to him.

"Hey, Paddle Boy." I smirk at him and slide into the seat.

"Um, yeah . . . they're *oars*, Leesie."

"Right. Right. Got it. Sorry. *Oar Boy.*"

"That's more like it." He hunches down and shoves his shoulder into mine. "Respect the sport, man. Respect the sport." He laughs and the group laughs with him. All of them. And in that moment, I am home. With a family. One that eats together, laughs together, body checks one another, and, in Eri's case, tells each other things they don't have to tell. Maybe even Luke is ready to embrace me as one of the family. I mean, he did smile at me just a second ago.

As the sound of laughter is replaced with chewing and forks scraping, I am already changing my mind. He did smile at me just a second ago? Did I seriously just think that? I am in charge here! Why do I continuously allow him to dictate the nature of our relationship? When he's all smiles, I am warm and fluttery. When he's dark and looming, I am ready to defend my life. No. Not on my watch, buddy. You will start batting *my* pitches. This is *my* inning. Okay. Take a couple of deep breaths. Don't look directly at anyone. Stay calm and collected.

Frances breaks me out of it by bringing up a calculus test we have on Thursday and a paper due Monday for AP English. Daisy and Eri offer their theories on how difficult the test will be given the short time we've spent on this unit while Patrick and Luke compare topics for their papers. I listen, nod, and comment now and then, but I am laying low for the rest of lunch. I am going to wait until Luke addresses me again, and if it's not in a way I like, I am going to call him on it. I don't have to wait long.

"So, Leesie, I know you said you ride, and I am going to the stables today. You want to come along?" Daisy has waited for a break in the schoolwork conversations to ask me, so it's quiet at the table, and now all eyes are fixed on me.

"I'd love that. Thanks. I miss the smell, actually. It's been a while."

"I know what you mean. It's only been a couple days for me, but I can't wait to get there today."

Patrick is back and forth, watching us like he is witnessing two people who just lapsed into a fit of speaking a foreign language, ancient Sanskrit or something.

"The *smell*? How does one miss the smell of manure and dirt and whatever else you find in a barn polluting our clean city air that's ripe with the scent of automobiles and French fries?"

"You wouldn't understand," Daisy and I say at the same time. We are both surprised to hear the other's voice mixed in with our own. We meet eyes, wide and understanding, sharing in something only farm people know, and we laugh.

"I'll drive you," Daisy says, letting out a last giggle. "Meet me at my car at the end of the day."

"Great." I'm all smiles. I don't remember what my real-life connection to horses is, but in the moment I don't care. I just know that for some reason I'm excited to get the chance to be around them.

"Can I come?" Eri's words break through the moment Daisy and I are having. Her words give a lot away. I know that by the look on Daisy's face. Daisy's taken aback, surprised, puzzled. This is her best friend, though, right? Why should she be surprised that Eri would want to come?

"Uh, sure, Eri. Of course you can come. You are always invited. I just thought, you know, that it's not your thing."

Eri glances around at everyone but Luke. Her shoulders are raised slightly. She is pointing the fork, prongs down, into her tray. She's tense.

"Maybe I haven't given it enough of a shot. I think I could come to enjoy it. Frances, how 'bout you? Make it a girl's day?"

She's deflecting. Nice try, Eri. Turn it into a girl's thing. Like that's your motivation. To make sure no girl is left out? I don't buy it. You didn't like it when it was just Daisy and me, that's all. Why not? You could have invited me somewhere when we're alone next period in art if you wanted me to yourself. Wait. That theory doesn't work because art hasn't happened yet. Maybe Eri *had* planned on that and Daisy had stolen her thunder. Or maybe Eri doesn't like to share her best friend unless it is a group thing. Or maybe the fact that she and Daisy don't share the animal husbandry thing and Daisy and I do makes her insecure. Okay, too many theories that make sense for me to come up with an answer.

"Sorry ladies, but I have Future Business Owners of America this afternoon. And a study date with the math club after that. I'll wait for the next girls' day invite, and hopefully that one will not contain farm animals. Sorry, Daisy, but those things are just too big."

Daisy and I laugh again, but it lacks the ease it had earlier. This nervous laughter is covering up the sideways glance Daisy gives Eri. The glance complete with raised eyebrows and an unsaid "What the heck are you doing?" Eri looks away and starts collecting her trash. Lunch is almost over. And then I realize Luke has been silent through all of this. I look over at him, and I see his tense, furrowed brow has returned. Man, this guy is all over the place! I am starting to think that he is unhinged. Is he angry? I won't get the answer to that question by reading his body language or waiting for him to speak because in the next second he is up with his tray and gone.

No one comments directly about Luke's departure. It's just Patrick who says, "Well, guys, I guess it's that time."

Daisy and Eri whisper on their way to the trash can. Frances has made the mental switch and is already in all-academic focus mode. Patrick throws out the trash for two cute girls at the next table, and I walk out of the dining hall alone. I walk to studio art not knowing what to expect when I see Eri. Apparently she's all surprises today.

Chapter

In addition to an opportunity for alone time with Eri, studio art has become a time for me to be creative and expressive without the constant scrutiny of someone watching. Eri doesn't ask to see what I'm working on, maybe because she doesn't want to have to reciprocate and share her work with me or maybe she respects my privacy, and the teacher doesn't hover. She says this is a time for creative artistic expression and that we should feel comfortable using our talents in whatever medium best cultivates them. Eri uses paint. I prefer to work with clay. I like the idea of being able to mold something into any likeness. I get to give it shape and design according to my plans. No rules, nothing forced, no missions, no Preceptors. Just me.

But Eri is in the mood to talk today.

"You excited for this afternoon?" she starts.

"Yeah, I am. You?" She'll know I am asking for an explanation when I redirect the question. She must know I want answers to the many questions lunch left us all with.

"Yes. I am. It's not my thing, true, but having you here, seeing you join in our activities so easily . . . it makes me rethink some of the things I never join in on. I live twenty minutes from the city, and yet I never cross the bridge just to be there, to walk around, to see the sights, to eat at a new place. And here Daisy has an interest I never experience with her. When I saw you so into it, I figured, why not? Maybe I should change things up, get out there more."

"Oh. Well, good. That's good. Well, what about you? Do you have any interests that the others don't join in on?" I have to find an interest of hers I can be into. I have to find a way to bond that is just about the two of us.

"Actually I do . . . I play the cello. My parents make me. It looks good on paper, you know. It's all about the résumé I'm building for my future successes and all that. At first I hated it, but now I think it's a chance for me to connect to sound in a way that most people don't. When the music is right, when the perfect note is struck, it's like the sound floats heavily in the room, circles me before it winds upward and then parts the skies. It's like it actually has to float to heaven because where else could a sound so beautiful go?"

She's angelic when she lets herself be. "That sounds amazing. I'd love to hear you play. I mean, who wouldn't want to watch sound come alive and part the heavens?"

"You'd be surprised. It doesn't have the same appeal as a crew meet on Boathouse Row or ten-thousand-dollar horses in a ritzy stable. . . ."

"Well, I'd love to hear you play. After the stables, maybe?"

She smiles now, "Okay. Sure. If you want to."

"I do."

We settle in to work. She is content now. Good. Now I just have to figure out what is eating Luke. I can't ask Eri. She never talks about Luke. They have some connection that remains top secret, off-limits to me. I can try to bump into him in the hallway or at the water fountain, but that doesn't seem likely. At the end of the day, though, I get my chance.

I walk out to the parking lot as soon as classes let out. I didn't see anyone else exit, but Luke is waiting at Daisy's car.

My heart beats faster; I curse my body for betraying me. *Calm. Collected. C'mon. He's not in control here.*

He's watching me walk over. *Of course. What else is new?*

I decide to play confident girl. Don't guys eat that up? I walk directly to him, never breaking stride, never slowing down, until I am inches from the car. I meet his stare and hold it. I break it only as I ease to his right, turning directly in front of him to take my place leaning beside him against the car. Our elbows are dangerously close to touching, and he senses it. He pulls his arm down straight to avoid it. I will not talk first. After all, I am taking control. Besides, I'm the one who is supposed to be at Daisy's car. What's he doing here?

But then he turns his head. And I feel him looking at me. And suddenly my knees are Jell-o-ey. *Play it off. Play it off.*

"Leesie . . ."

Why does my name sound so good when he says it?

"Leesie."

This time I turn my head and raise my chin slightly. I let him have a view of my face for a second before I lift my eyes to meet his. *There you go. Make him wait.*

I am making him wait, but I am also thinking of how to answer. I can't say, "What?" That's standoffish and slightly rude. I don't want him to change his mind if he wants to talk to me about something. I can't say, "Yes?" That is too passive and dumb-girlish. In the end I go with the only response that makes sense to me. A play for a play. This is my inning after all.

"Luke," I say. I see his chest rise slightly as he watches me say his name. He sucks in air and clenches his jaw.

This is now the second time we are deadlocked in a staring contest, only this time we have uttered each other's name. What is this thing? He's not doing anything. He's not saying anything. He isn't making a face. He isn't smiling or smirking; he's just looking at me. Into my eyes.

In an instant I can almost see him change his mind about talking to me. He's lost somewhere in the moment. His eyes dance over my face, and then his serious stare becomes playful.

"Leesie," he says again. He turns the corners of his mouth up a bit.

"Luke," I raise my eyebrows slightly and smirk. I leave my lips parted.

"Have fun on the farm today."

"I will, thanks."

"Leesie!" Daisy interrupts. "You ready for this? I'm so glad you're coming!" She bounds over to the car. Eri is a step behind.

Luke and I break our gaze and turn toward the girls. Eri mouths something to Luke that I can't catch. I look back at Luke in time to see him shake his head no.

No? No, what? Was he supposed to tell me something?

"I'll see you ladies later." Luke gives a general wave and turns away. I wait to see if he'll brush past me. You know, the whole accidentally-on-purpose-touching guys do that they don't think girls know about. But nothing. Not even an over-the-shoulder look as he walks away. I stare after him for a minute until reality comes back to me. In my reality, I don't watch boys walk away or hope for a second look or a random brush-against. No. That's their job. I hate how I have to keep reminding myself of my own rules. This guy is jumbling everything up.

"Well, get in already! We're missing the prime time! Perfect weather, perfect breeze, nice and sunny—let's go!"

Daisy's enthusiasm is infectious, and by the time we pull out of the parking lot, I am ready for this trip. I can't wait to see the fields, the riding ring, the barn, and the pastures.

Saanan Stables is only a ten-minute drive south. I love how within minutes of driving down the main road out of Preston, we're on full-blown country roads. No sidewalks, no streetlights. Open fields for miles. The only crop we pass that I can name is corn, but the fields are filled with so much green that I'm sure there isn't a salad ingredient missing out here. We slow down through a blinking yellow light. There isn't even enough traffic to warrant an operating traffic light. The only time we have a blinking light in the city is when there's a power failure or an accident, and the blinking light usually results in another accident or at least a lot of beeping and profanity.

"Here we are!" Daisy announces as we make a right onto a dirt driveway. It winds us past a house and a vegetable garden and down to an unpainted barn with the words *Saanan Stables* etched into the wood above the double doors. One of the doors is open, and inside I see the stalls, some with horses' heads poking out of them. As I get out of the car, I take a deep breath. Deeper than I have in a long time. And it smells good. The way the manure and alfalfa mix together to make a smell that screams nature is something I could never describe to someone who thinks it stinks. Heck, I can't describe it to anyone, considering I don't even have the memories as to why I love this stuff in the first place. All I know is I do. I love it. A peaceful feeling washes over me that I don't remember feeling before. Maybe I felt this way back in my real life, but since I have been with Tobias and on missions, I have never felt this way. I close my eyes and lift my face to the sky and take another deep breath. I let the sounds of the farm play in my ears—the whinnies, the bleating of sheep and goats in the distance, the sound of hooves crunching gravel.

"Leesie, you okay?" Eri asks.

I open my eyes and turn to her, "I'm fine. Just soaking it all in. I could live out here. Right here, in this barn. Forever."

"Really? You love it that much? You must miss it at your aunt's house, then."

"Right. My aunt's house. I do." I'm not even effectively lying right now. I am too caught up in this moment to think about the lies of my constructed past handed to me by Tobias. I am caught up in the fact that something about this atmosphere is directly connected to my real life and to who I really am. As at peace as I am here, I am furious at the fact that I don't even get to know *why* I am at peace.

Daisy leads us into the barn. We pass a chestnut mare and two Arabian geldings before she stops in front of a stall.

"This is Jackson," she says like a proud mom. She steps to the side to allow us a full view, and he is magnificent. He's a palomino quarter horse. His dark-blond body is only slightly more golden than Daisy's hair, and his mane and tail, white blond, are like Daisy's highlights. They make a nice pair. I watch her let him nuzzle her. He bows his head and leans into her. She cups the space between his eyes and his ears and holds him like he's an overblown football. They make noises to each other until Daisy gives in and pushes him up. He has found the stash of baby carrots in her jacket pocket and won't stop nudging her. She pulls out a carrot and feeds it to him as she plays with his bottom lip.

"I'm just going to look around, Daisy. I want to see what else is in here."

"Okay. I'll get him saddled. Eri, do you want to watch?" I hear Eri's hesitant "yes" as I make my way down the stalls. I pass a couple of ponies. One is a beautiful dapple gray. Super old. His name is Norman Fellerman. Funny. A first and last name for a horse. A head down at the end catches my eye, and I turn from Norman. Two pricked ears are turned toward me, and a neigh catches me off guard.

She's a lovely Morgan mare. Dark brown, glistening. Her mane and tail are the same color as her body. She's sleek and beautiful. She looks expensive. I check out her nameplate. Mountain Swiss Starflower's Cleo. That's a heck of a name.

"Hello, Cleo. Do you go by Cleo?"

She shakes her tail, knocking off a few flies. She jerks her head up and stamps a foot twice. She wants me closer. She wants more attention, more talking to. I take another step towards her. Her head is inches from mine. She lowers it to my pockets, investigating. I reach up instinctively and put my hand out flat under her nose. She feels around for treats, and as she does, I blow a short breath over her. *Let her have your scent. Let her know you,* I hear in my ears. I know I have never been here before, but something is all too familiar. Someone gave me advice, taught me how to behave around horses. Taught me to love it here. To love them. Who? My parents? Did I grow up on a farm?

I back away from Cleo to look at her. I need a second to process this. I start at her eyes and move to her ears, which are changing direction from facing forward to pointing out to the side. Not back—that's good. She's interested in me, wants me here. And how do I know that you can read a horse by its ears? I guess ears back is common knowledge. I mean, dogs do it, too. I move my eyes down her neck to her withers. Am I supposed to know that the bones at the base of her neck are called withers? Is that common knowledge? I watch her shift her weight from left hind foot to right. She's shoed. Should I notice that? She's been clipped; all the stray hairs around her hocks and muzzle are neatly trimmed. I shouldn't know that, right? What does it matter? My gut tells me I have been here before. Not in this barn, but in a barn, in every nook and cranny of a barn. I have mucked stalls, I bet. I have fed and watered the horses, groomed them, handled their tack, saddled them. I can feel it. I *know* I have.

I leave Cleo with one last stroke down her neck and walk out of the barn to find Daisy, Eri, and Jackson.

Eri is standing to the left of Jackson's head. Daisy is tightening the girth on his saddle. She has changed into English-style riding pants and boots. She looks the part. But, with her white T-shirt tucked in instead of a straight-collared blouse, she makes what could appear pretentious look natural and casual. I can't get over how well she wears her money. There really is something so easy about her. She's not snobby or high-maintenance. I like her more and more each time I am around her.

"There you are! Did you meet anyone you liked inside?" Daisy greets happily.

"I saw Mr. Fellerman. And Cleo."

"Norman is a hoot! He's old, but he's still got his personality. And Cleo, well, she's spectacular. She's the owner's daughter's horse."

"Yes, she's lovely. I think she liked me."

"Did she? Well, she's picky. You must have good horse sense then, from all that time at your aunt's stables."

"Yeah, I guess so."

"Well, girls, I am going to walk him over. Do you want to meet at the riding ring? I'll warm him up, and then if either of you would like to hop on, well, you just say so!"

Eri and I watch her walk Jackson away from the barn. She looks so graceful. He looks so content. We turn left and walk to the ring. There are seats in front of the ring, and as we sit, we see her enter from the other side. She mounts him once one of the barn hands closes the gate. Daisy leans forward, wraps her arms, reins in hand, around his neck, and whispers in his ear. He flicks his ears toward her in response. She straightens up and adjusts her feet in the stirrups. They start out at a walk.

"It's beautiful, isn't it? Horse and rider?" I ask her.

"Yes. You must miss it."

"I do. I miss a lot of things."

Neither Eri nor I ride this afternoon. We watch Daisy. Cheer her on. Like she cheered Patrick. We just sit and are with her. With each other. And when Jackson has been lovingly put back in his stall after many more treats and strokes and kind words, we head to Eri's, where I look forward to giving her the same thing: a cheering section. And maybe, maybe if I learn to be someone's audience, someone will want to be mine someday. Not because of a forced connection, not because of a mission, but because I have real people who want to be my friends, my family.

Chapter
14

As I sit in the backseat of Daisy's car, I look out at the farms we passed only a few hours ago. I see them differently now. Now I see everything as a possible trigger for memories that might come back. Flashes of something I used to know or may have experienced with people who were mine. Tobias said it could happen as my skills improve.

Suddenly my mission is not my only focus. I will continue to pursue my relationship with Eri, but I will also focus on myself. Who was I when I was just a girl with a family?

Since I found Tobias, I have been someone with a lot of catching up to do. So much time had been lost. I was so late in connecting with my Preceptor. I had so much learning to do, Tobias said. I should have accomplished so many missions by now, Tobias said. And so I threw myself into my work. I had so much expected of me, being the type of Seer that I am. Tobias said someone with my gift could complete the missions that other Seers could not because they cannot Extract or move memories. Tobias said he knew I could complete them. That's why he sent me, on my first mission, into the mind of someone mentally sick. Other Seers can only look around. Like the spectators at a circus, they can watch the lions perform, but only the lion tamer is in the ring touching and manipulating those potentially dangerous creatures. I am the lion tamer.

Every mission Tobias had sent me on has required an increasingly difficult amount of research and trust building, and the Navigations themselves have become more intricate. How did he know I could do it? How did he know that I would be able to focus on missions only and put aside any desire I have to figure out where I came from and how I got to him? Is he just counting on me staying focused? Is that why I go from mission to mission, bouncing around from one school to the next, one group of friends to the next, never cultivating any real relationships for myself? Am I worth more as a Seer if I am *only* a Seer, *only an Extractor,* and not a real person, too?

"You're quiet back there. You have a good time?" Daisy asks, interrupting my string of questions to which I have no answers.

"I had a great time. Thanks for inviting me. It felt good to be around horses again," I say, wishing I knew why it had felt that way.

"Sure. Anytime. I go to the stables at least three days a week. You're always welcome."

Daisy pulls into Eri's driveway a few minutes later. Eri had walked to school today. She lives a few blocks down and walks if the weather is nice. Daisy won't be staying. She's got to get cleaned up and a jump on homework and prepare for her calculus test on Thursday. It'll just be Eri and me. This is what I have been waiting for.

Eri's house is sprawling. A picket fence borders the sidewalk from the front lawn, and a curved slate walkway beckons us to the front door. The grass is lush, and a blooming cherry tree and varying colors of shrubs and flowering plants complete a picture fit for a postcard. The house is painted a cream color with accent colors of gray and navy. It has a cedar roof and a grand dark-wood front door. Eri continues around the house, though, to a side door, a more modest entryway, and pulls out her key. "My parents aren't home yet."

She doesn't offer an explanation for their absence. Are they always home late? It's going on six, so it's not too late, but do they eat dinner together? Do they spend time with one another in the evenings? Is she alone every day?

"Oh. When do they usually get home?" I ask.

"Seven thirty most nights." She walks through a mud room that is nicer than and almost half the size of my entire apartment.

"Who makes you dinner?"

"My meals are prepared for me by a chef my parents have on staff. He comes in the afternoon and cooks for us, then leaves it. I have to wait for them to get here to eat. We have a must-dine-together rule," she explains.

"Well, at least you never have to eat alone," I answer, attempting to keep her positive. I don't want her to get too moody and brooding to the point where she doesn't want to talk about it anymore, but I didn't think my comment through well enough.

"Oh, I'm so sorry! Here I am complaining about family time when you eat alone all the time. Or do you?"

We're in the kitchen now. She has stopped leading me through the house and turns to face me.

"No, that's okay. I didn't mean it like that. I didn't mean it to sound like I was telling you to be thankful for what you have. I hate when people do that. Just because you want to complain, doesn't mean you think you have it worse than anybody else. And I don't feel bad for myself, so you shouldn't tiptoe around what to say to me. Tobias works late. I usually eat alone. But I like it okay. Seriously . . . complain."

She laughs. "I don't mean to. I just can't—I mean, look at all this!" She gestures around the fanciest kitchen I have ever seen. It opens up to a family room. A formal dining room is off to the left, and what looks like a formal living room is off to the right. Marble tiles everywhere, lots of leather, a grand piano peaking at us from the living room.

"It's beautiful."

"It's a lot."

"A lot of stuff? A lot of what?"

"A lot to live up to. What if I don't want this? I mean, I guess everybody wants money, but I don't want to work as hard as my parents do. I don't want the years of schooling past high school and training abroad and the hours they keep and the stuffy parties and the fake friends and the social obligations. What are social obligations, anyway? They're just fancy words for *behave like everyone else*, and *keep up with the neighbors*. How do you tell your ultra-successful parents you just don't feel like working as hard as they do? That sounds so pathetic, doesn't it? I might as well say, 'Mom, Dad, I would like your permission to be a lazy slob when I grow up, please. Thanks.'" She presses her palms down on the granite countertop.

To keep her gushing, I have to make sure there is nothing

about my face that says I am judging her or remotely disturbed by her emotional outburst. "What kind of life do you want, Eri?"

She softens. Most people do when they feel validated, and when you add their name at the end of a question. I don't know why the name thing works, but it does.

"I just want time to figure it out. With parents on the fast track, there is never any time. Every goal has an age by which it should be reached. I just feel like I can't breathe sometimes."

"What are you going to do? Can you talk to your parents? Tell them how suffocated you feel?"

"Are you kidding? Never! My dad is already hovering around more. Quite honestly I can't believe he's not here. He's been standing over me, asking for updates on my grades, coming to my academic competitions—which he never did before—and then telling me I need to be more aggressive, stand out more. He leaves me brochures for leadership councils and women's academic fellowship retreats and performing opportunities. He won't leave me alone! If I tell him I want time to relax, he may have a stroke. According to him, I am not working hard enough as it is!"

"What do you think you need to tell him in order to get him to back off?"

This is the magic question, the one that is the key to my mission. I need to know what she wants with her life right now and in the future. I need to find out what is holding her back, and I need to know why she believes her father's incessant involvement in her life is causing her to perform below her potential at school. And then I need to Navigate Dr. Kuono to find out what is at the center of his suffocation of Eri. Once in, I believe I can manipulate Dr. Kuono's memories in a way that will relieve whatever pressures he can't help but place on Eri's shoulders. And then, according to Tobias, Arashi Kuono can get back to whatever fabulous breakthrough he's working on, the one that will, apparently, change the world of Seers as we know it and maybe get me some answers about myself in the process.

"I don't know, Leesie. I don't know. Right now, I just need to forget about it."

She turns and walks through the family room and up the stairs. I follow her up and through the third door on the left. A music room, by the looks of it. It has an upright piano—I guess the baby grand downstairs is for company—several guitars, a violin, the cello, and table covered in sheet music. There are several chairs with music stands in front of them set up under a cluster of windows, and against the opposite wall is a loveseat. For the audience, I assume.

I take my seat and wait.

Eri sits in the chair behind the cello, grabs the bow, and turns a few pages of sheet music. She tucks the chunk of hair that always creeps over her cheekbone behind her ear. I close my eyes. I don't know why, but after hearing her description of the sound this thing is going to make, I figure I should get in the moment. And she's right. It is beautiful.

I lean my head back against the wall and take a deep breath. The sound, the tearful moaning coming from her cello, by her hands, is the single most freeing tone I have ever heard. I am twirling to the music. In my head, I am flying, soaring over land and water that once held me captive. I am moved by the way the low notes reverberate in the pit of my stomach and the high notes make my eyes sting. I am moved by the fact that I am physically moved. She was right. This is the music of the heavens.

I open my eyes to watch her. She sways gracefully at times. Then, when the music gets more intense, she frowns, and her movements are jerky and forced. She is somewhere else, though. She looks more relaxed than I have ever seen her, and yet more intense than ever.

She puts her bow down and looks up at me.

"Eri, that was everything you said it was. The most beautiful sound I've heard."

"Oh, thanks. I'm glad you liked it." She fumbles with the music again. She seems all at once a little self-conscious and unsure again.

"Eri, I know I don't have the answers for you and I wish I could fix it all, but can I just say that while you play, it seems like you are pretty free. I mean, what if you focused more of your time on your music? Maybe that would help."

"It does. And I do. I use it as an escape. But it has been invaded. It's not mine anymore. It's now something that I compete with. Performances all over the East Coast and a bunch more coming up."

"Oh."

"Look, thanks, Leesie. It means a lot to me that you came and you listened and now you are trying to help. And the truth is, I will be fine. How many people would die for my problems?"

"Don't do that. Don't convince yourself that because you don't have it as bad as so many others, you can't want more. Sure, there are tons of people with heart-wrenching problems that you or I would never make it through, but everyone has a right to want something else, to want something more. You just have to make sure you never complain to the wrong people. Like someone struggling to make ends meet would not want to hear about your fear of the constraints of success."

She laughs. "Yeah. You're right."

Eri gets up and walks toward me. She has a we-better-get-on-with-our-individual-evenings look on her face. She knows her parents are coming home soon and is obviously not into the idea of my staying to meet them. I do have to gain access to Dr. Kuono, and soon, but I am not ready yet. I need to know what Eri wants, what she needs from her father to be happy and content. Scratch that. I need to know what she needs In order to jump on the fast track. I need to know what will spark a drive in her that will enable Dr. Kuono to back off of her and get back to focusing on work. If I don't manipulate the memory that will transform Eri's father into what she needs him to be in order for her to be successful, the cycle will just continue to repeat itself. And my mission will never end.

But then again, I could stay.

As soon as the thought creeps into my head, I have to shove it away. This is exactly what Tobias says I have to work on. I am not supposed to be getting over-involved, over-attached. I am supposed to get in, complete my mission, and get out. I cannot afford to forget that.

Seers do not remain with their mission subjects. And they do not abandon a mission. The Seer would be ostracized. A target of outrage from the entire Seer operation. Considering I have no family, no one else, and this Seer community is all I've got, that's a lot to lose. Not to mention the supreme loyalty Seers have to their Preceptors. Once a connection is made between Seer and Preceptor, that bond is to come first.

"I better get some homework done before they come home. He'll probably ask to see it or spend the rest of the evening watching me study."

"Sounds like a blast. Yeah, I better get to work, too. I had an awesome day today, Eri. You and Daisy are quite the talents," I say as I head down the stairs towards the main foyer.

"Thanks." She holds the front door open for me. "Leesie?"

I step down and turn to her.

"You're a good person."

Huh? Where'd that come from?

"Um . . . thanks?" I give her a look that should tell her I have no idea where she's going with this.

She smiles. Backs up. And closes the door.

Okay, well, all right, then. Am I destined to be left with nothing but a ton of questions after I hang out with these people? What gives, man?

The walk up Delaware Ave. back to the academy should offer the perfect opportunity to clear my head. It is such a beautiful night, the perfect no-jacket night with just the right light breeze. The sky is clear and full of stars. As I walk past beautiful home after beautiful home, I wish this were my neighborhood. I wish, again, that I could stay here. So much for shoving that thought away.

I pass the front of the academy and turn after its left wing to the student parking lot. Mine is the only vehicle remaining. I am caught up in how much I love the look of my truck when I notice something that shouldn't be there. A figure? Is someone leaning against my truck? The figure turns to face me. Oh, crap. Not now. It's Luke.

Chapter

What is this? Is his special gift knowing when to lean against a vehicle until I show up? No. Obviously I would show up at Daisy's car. We had plans. And my truck? I'd say it's a safe bet that I'd be here sooner or later to claim it. So he wanted to be sure he saw me before I went home. Before tomorrow. Why?

No better way to find out than to ask him.

I walk around the front end to the side he's leaning on.

"Hey," I start.

"Hey." He's trying to read me, gauge how I feel about his being here. And why wouldn't he be unsure about how I would take it? He's in an empty school parking lot waiting for me against the *driver side* door of my vehicle. So I can't even jump in and take off. It's dark and he's waiting for a girl like some kind of psycho stalker. Sure, I feel great about this.

"What are you doing here?" I ask.

"I wanted to see how today went," he says, looking my face over, reading me still.

"How today went? You're on my truck because you want to know how my afternoon at the farm went?"

"You went to Eri's after, didn't you?"

I have to get to the bottom of this Luke and Eri thing.

"Yes. She played the cello for me," I answer matter-of-factly as I watch him frowning.

"Did she tell you anything?"

He is really grilling me. What the heck does he think of me? That I have some ulterior motive? That I don't truly care about Eri? Well, I do have a motive, but that doesn't mean I can't have her best interests in mind, which I believe this mission does.

"Like what?" I am playing dumb all the way. If he wants information from me, he is going to have to work for it.

"Did she talk about her parents? Her dad?"

He doesn't seem to like that I am defensive and tight-lipped. His voice is pinched, and his body is tensing up even more if that's possible.

"She talked about a bunch of things, Luke. I didn't realize I had to report a play-by-play to you if I spend time with Eri in your absence. Did I sign some sort of contract that I am not aware of? Did I not get the memo?"

I know giving him attitude could be dangerous, considering how hot and bothered he is right now, but I have a limit to how much annoyance I can take before I lash out and want to blow someone's hair back. But it has the opposite effect. He suddenly becomes aware of me. That I am a person. One who will challenge him if I have to. It's like before he was talking to me as a subject, someone lower than he is on some level.

Luke answers me after a deep breath that smooths his brow and relaxes his shoulders. "Leesie, I just worry about her. She is so undecided right now. And you're confident. Strong. I was worried you might tell her to fight her father's wishes. That you would tell her to fight for what she wants. Only I am not sure she knows what that is yet. Or that she is strong enough to fight for herself. She's so sensitive to how others feel. I don't think she is the type of person who can challenge people regardless of how it may hurt them."

Strong, confident? Thanks. The type of person who can challenge people regardless of how it may hurt them? Does he think that of me? Am I that type of person?

"Are you saying I would try to convince her to do that? To hurt her family? I don't have one, so how could I possibly have any idea how to respect the feelings of its members? Is that it?"

I don't really believe he thinks that of me. I haven't been cold or unfeeling in the short time that I have been a member of this group. But I want him to back all the way off. I want him to see me as someone with my own set of feelings and sensitivity. Maybe I want to appear a little vulnerable. Just a little . . . but why? So that it might occur to him to protect me instead of Eri? Is that it? Am I jealous of how attentive he is to her? But then I think of having someone traipsing all over town scowling at people and interrogating them on my behalf. Gag me. I would throw up. I'd rip my own eyelashes out before I'd allow someone to guard-dog me.

"I don't think that. I don't. I'm sorry—" He leans toward me slightly. His eyes are pleading now. He doesn't want to insult me. I can see that.

Fine. He doesn't think I am cold and heartless. He just worries about his friend being influenced by her strong, confident, and ultra-wise new friend. Okay, Luke. You can have some answers.

"She talked about her dad, yes. I asked her what she needed to be content and happy. She couldn't answer. She played her cello for me. I left. I offered her nothing. No advice. Frankly, I don't have any answers or suggestions to give. I don't know what she should do."

Yet.

But once I figure out the answers, I will be fixing her father for her, so don't worry, Lukie. I've got this.

"Oh. Okay. And, look, I'm sorry about all this. This ambush. I was going to say something to you about it this afternoon, but I got distracted. And then Eri was there, wondering what I was doing. It just didn't go the way it was supposed to go."

"No?"

I make eye contact and hold it as I say this. I want him to acknowledge the moment we shared this afternoon. The great name exchange. Was that something to him? It was surely something to me.

"No. I got . . . caught up. . . ."

He's all mine now. He is definitely not thinking about Eri anymore.

"Caught up in what?"

I'm totally leading him. Like a lagging dog on a leash.

"In you."

There's that deep breathing again. His chest rises and falls. His jaw clenches. But he makes no move toward me. He remains leaning forward, turned toward me with his butt and right hand on my truck. I am facing him. My left hand rests on my truck too, dangerously close to his.

I give it another second, leaving his words lingering out there. But still he doesn't move toward me. No touch. No kiss.

"I better let you get home."

And that's it. He looks past me, drops his hand from my truck without so much as brushing mine, straightens up, and walks away.

"I'll see you tomorrow," he calls with his back to me.

I don't bother to answer. I will not talk to a guy's back. You walk away, that's it. No more conversation for you. What's worse is my little power play is pointless anyway. Like he cares if I didn't answer him. He walked away! He is obviously done with me for the night. This guy is infuriating. His intensity is unpredictable. He is hot and cold. He is toying with me.

But truth be told? I like it more and more all the time.

Chapter

I drive aggressively on the way home, taking out my frustrations on the highway. I am determined to control something right now. My speed, who's in front of me, which route I'll take. I am currently controlling so little in my life that I am reduced to this. Eri is still a mystery. My relationship with Luke grows more and more complicated. I have to constantly worry about reporting to Tobias. I need to sit in my chair and sketch out a plan.

Once in my apartment, I lay my book bag down by the door. Homework will wait until I clear my head. I pour a glass of water, grab a bag of soy crisps and my journal, and cross the kitchen to my chair. The night is clear and noisy. I hear the honking of a horn, the barking of a dog, and the scratchy voice of a guy yelling on the street below before I settle into my usual position. I maneuver the throw pillow into the right corner. My left elbow finds its place, half on the pillow, half on the arm of the chair. My left leg bends, knee up, heel down on the seat. My other leg remains on the hardwood floor, but I tilt my foot to the side, bending at the ankle so that the outside of my foot feels the smooth, cool wood. I open the bag of soy crisps—always the same cheddar flavor—and place the bag in my lap. My water is on the windowsill to my left so that I have to extend my already supported left arm only a couple of inches to grab it. I reach into the bag with my right hand only.

For the first time I seemingly float outside of myself, watching this. Realizing the extent to which I am a creature of habit. I am almost robotic. A droid. Programmed to follow the same patterns of behavior, the same movements to achieve the same result every time. No wonder this ever-changing Luke and Eri thing is bothering me so badly. I can't even sit in a chair without turning it into a process of repetition. I allow myself to assess this further. I need to get to the root of my discontent. What is really bothering me about this mission?

As I record the facts of the day, I think on my previous missions. Even though the faces changed, the schools were different, and the information I was searching for was never the same, the one constant was the fact that I knew I was getting in, getting information, and Navigating for a desired result. Then getting out. There is a comfort in that. I was in a routine. The down changed but I was still running the same play. Somehow in the constant upheaval I found a pattern that made me feel secure. Now, with this mission, it's not only a different down; it's a whole new play, one that I haven't rehearsed for.

I am supposed to be running this show. In my other missions I always felt like the director on the set. I commanded my actors' performances and worked them according to my desired result. After all, I am in control of the level to which these mission relationships develop. Aren't I?

I feel a pang in my chest. That's it—I'm getting close to the root of the problem. I feel like Luke repeatedly wields the upper hand. And Eri. I should be getting the dish from her by now. She should be telling me her innermost secrets and every detail about the problems she is having with her father. The more time I spend with her, the closer I feel to her, and the more I learn about her. But it's always on her terms. She let me into her musical world today by opening up about the cello and playing for me, but she has yet to truly open up about her dad.

And then a final thought, a last tugging as if the clouds of confusion part, and I see the center of my problem. I see what I have been too confused or too busy to see.

What will Navigating Eri's dad really do? Even if I can get her father to back off, it will never really end for her. Sure, he may let her have a little more breathing room, but he is never going to say, "Sure, honey, just be yourself and anything you want is okay." No. Dr. Arashi Kuono is always going to want his only daughter to achieve professionally. He is never going to stop pushing. So that leaves me with a gaping question. Why am I on this mission? Why has it not occurred to the other Seers that this mission's success is too subjective? Sure I can Navigate Dr. Kuono to find the root of why he pressures Eri, but that does not mean that he will stop being involved in her life, stop caring about her success, stop wanting the best for her. It makes sense to assume then that I am the only one who measures the success of this mission by Eri's comfort level. Tobias is only concerned with Dr. Kuono getting back to his work.

None of this would be a problem if I didn't like Eri. Or the rest of them. I like them. I've broken Tobias's rule: don't get attached. And now I've taken it one step further by admitting to myself that I am attached. That's so much worse. I am not even denying it to myself anymore.

Even without proper reference to help me gauge my feelings for people I know, I feel connected to Eri, and I'm infatuated (yeah, I may as well admit that, too) with Luke. So I have broken the rules. No. I have torn up the rule book and set it on fire.

Like the loud popping of a splitting log on a fire, three sharp knocks at the door jerk me to attention. I hurry to finish my entry. I add a few details to my bulleted list of things I did during my time at Eri's house. Satisfied, I stand, stretch, inhale deeply, and attempt to remove any trace of care or concern from my face before I open the door. I follow Daniel obediently to Tobias and decide to keep my thoughts on Eri's role in this mission a secret. I know the lecture my sentiment toward her will receive.

When I enter Tobias's office, his chair is already facing the door. He is waiting for me.

"Good evening, Elise."

"Hello, Tobias."

I cross the room quickly and set my journal inches from his hands.

"A prosperous day?"

"Yes. It was."

He fingers the bookmarked page and motions for me to proceed as he begins to read.

"I secured an invitation to Eri's home today."

"I see. Very good. And what information did you gather?"

"She is overwhelmed by the successes of her parents. She is worried that the life they have laid out will not satisfy her."

"How so? Does she not desire to be financially secure and respected in the field of her choosing?"

"I think she does. I just think she worries that it will force her into a world of long hours and forced friendships. She seems worried she will lose herself."

"How can she worry she will lose herself if she already cannot find her way?"

Tobias likes to speak in riddles. If his spoken word were printed sentences, they would appear on the page as circles instead of lines. He says things that are thought-provoking but only further question what has already been asked. I can never respond to these riddles, though Tobias never waits for my response.

"You seem to be weighing her thoughts and concerns heavily."

I must have used the words "I think" too many times. My concern for her is what I want to hide. Again I don't respond.

"Elise, it is time to move beyond Ms. Kuono. Think of her father. Think of his thoughts, *his* concerns. The sooner you complete this mission, the sooner not only his daughter but Dr. Kuono will be at ease as well."

"Yes."

Tobias slides the journal out to my edge of the desk.

"Do you have plans in place for tomorrow?"

"I have some ideas."

Tobias draws the corners of his eyes toward his nose ever so slightly. That was the wrong answer.

"We need progress on this. Calculate a move. See that you turn away from Ms. Kuono's whims and toward Dr. Kuono's work."

"I will."

As Tobias rotates away from me, I grab my journal and exit quickly. I have escaped a lecture, but his displeasure is evident enough.

Back in the safety of my apartment, I know I should tackle my homework, shower, and then get some needed sleep. But I can't. Tobias made it clear that tomorrow has to be pivotal. So instead, I head over to my chair.

What can I do to get around Luke's protective watch and convince Eri to open up? What about tomorrow will be different from today? I had the perfect opportunity today. Luke wasn't around. I had Eri to myself. I was in her house. Still . . . no answers. I would need a perfect situation. It would have to be a moment of closeness where the two of us could bond about something, and she would feel comfortable enough and have enough time to open up. How can I be sure she will want to hang out again tomorrow? And what are the chances, if we don't get together after school, that we will have time for a talk in between classes? This could be impossible. This would need a miracle or something.

Or something.

Wait. Couldn't I make a connection happen? Couldn't I make it so that she can't help but give me the answers I know I need? Couldn't I Navigate her?

Could I? I feel my stomach bottom out as the idea sets in. It's risky. It's not technically part of the mission. When Tobias spelled out the nature of missions before he sent me on my first one, I likened mission rules to those of contract killing. A hit man has a subject he is after. He is not cleared to kill all who stand in his way. Limit the casualties. Make few waves. Missions have a target. Seers are not cleared to Navigate everyone associated with that target. I have been cleared to Navigate Dr. Kuono. But Navigating Eri would get me information quickly. And Tobias made it clear that his clock is ticking.

I wake up the next morning before my alarm. I remember feeling clear and determined when I went to bed. I had a think session in my chair, came to a few realizations and a solution, and felt good about it. Now as I lie in the dark, willing myself to get up, I feel queasy and full of dread. Can I do it? Can I Navigate Eri? Today?

In the shower I let the water cascade over me like a warm blanket. I fold into it and let it hold me. I imagine it as a bear hug or when I see a toddler, arms around her father's knees, him arching down and over. The father's hug is like a crested wave.

I dress without bothering to take note of what I'm wearing. Some sort of jeans and shirt combination. But I blow-dry my hair with care. I sit on the edge of my bed, put my chest on my knees, and let my hair hang almost to the floor. I scrunch it and mold the curls. I don't know why my hair has the power to change my mood and help me, but I know when I feel it surround me it becomes my shield, a mask, when I want to reinvent myself, and a cloak when I want to hide. It will be my shield today.

In my truck I am distracted. I cross the Ben Franklin Bridge into New Jersey without remembering having taken the exit off 95 toward the bridge let alone crossing it. I look in the rearview mirror and see a stream of cars making headway and starting to move into the next lane to pass me. I realize I am barely doing the speed limit. I have to get it together. I have to be sharper than this. Eri is smart, and Luke never misses anything. If I am off this morning, they will notice.

I pull into my usual space in the academy parking lot. The vision of Luke against my truck floods my brain. In an instant I am next to him again. Again the air is thick with tension and whatever else we create between us. I inhale deeply and glance at my knuckles. They are white as I grip the steering wheel. My shoulders are hunched, and I am lurching forward. How long have I been in this tense, unnatural position? I flex my hands and arch my back in an attempt to unfold. My back is stiff and my hands tingle. No wonder I can't focus my brain. I can't even control my body.

The sight of Patrick breaks me out of it.

"Hey, Lees!"

Patrick is slinging a bag over his shoulder. I am glad it's Patrick I see first. There is something easy and calming about him. Maybe it's his steady smile or his constant positivity. Whatever it is, I am thankful for it. It's exactly what I need.

"Morning, Patrick."

"Looking ravishing as usual. Ready for the test?"

His mantra is always the same. Compliment and connect. I know the trick. And yet I fall for it every time.

"Thanks," I say as I slide my hair off my shoulder with my

free hand, "and you're looking pretty fine yourself."

Patrick beams. One thing I know: people who dish out the compliments do so because secretly they cannot get enough of them for themselves. He doesn't say anything, just smiles big enough for his dimples to show.

"I'm ready for the test. You?" I ask as we fall in line beside each other.

"Ready and willing . . ."

Enough people have arrived that Patrick has to stop often to address his adoring fans. Shouts of "Never looked better! Love the shirt—is it new?" and my personal favorite, "There she is!" are called down the hall to our quirky, charismatic English teacher, who clearly looks forward to Patrick's daily greetings.

We part ways to our homerooms, but I am happy to feel that his infectious confidence has had lasting effects. I feel better, more resolved. I remind myself that gaining the information I need by Navigating Eri will benefit both of us. If only I can get past the fact that I feel like I am betraying her.

I spend the rest of the morning focusing extra attention on assignments and lectures in order to pass the day. I need to get through lunch and get to art. Art is the ideal opportunity. No Luke. No hulking teacher. It's just the two of us sitting across from each other. Perfect.

I make it through the morning, but at the sound of the bell for lunch, I tense. With each step toward the dining hall, my gut tightens into a ball of rubber bands, wound around and around each other into a pointless mass. This knot is not about Eri. This is about Luke.

This theme of us leaving each other at the height of emotional tension is causing us to start each subsequent meeting at a higher and higher point. We're not idling anymore. We're revving engines, waiting for the checkered flag to wave.

As I head toward the table where everyone is already sitting, I notice he's watching me. I'm less bothered by the fact that his eyes are fixed on me; I'm getting used to it. I am bothered by the fact that I cannot read his face. He doesn't have the angry, kill-me stare he used to give me. But he doesn't look like he plans on pulling a bouquet of roses from behind his back either.

The rest of the group is chatting casually as I sit down.

"So what was the answer to the last question?" Daisy is leaning toward Frances, sliding a piece of paper toward her. Frances makes a feeble attempt at another bite of her turkey salad sandwich, but Daisy is now armed with a pencil and is asking for a re-creation.

"Daisy, let the girl eat!" Eri playfully shoves Daisy away from Frances. Frances is all smiles. Everyone at the table knows she would sacrifice food for the sake of feeding brains any day.

I can blend right into the scene. Having taken the math test already, I actually am interested in the lesson Frances is giving us. Plus I can avoid Luke's gaze without being obvious. By the time lunch is over, I have learned a couple things: Luke doesn't bother to talk to me when the others are around, I am too focused on Eri right now to care, and I did fairly well, according to Frances, on the math test.

As usual Luke sets Eri's pace as they leave the dining hall at the end of lunch. I trail behind and watch them all. Patrick is complimenting a group of girls, who giggle and swoon in his wake. Daisy is laughing with her mouth open and head thrown back in her easy, confident way. Frances is a walking advertisement to her fellow students for assuming the role of a serious student. Even Luke and Eri look at ease as they walk, heads close, in conversation. I take in all of their quirks, funny faces, and starkly different personalities. Though I haven't had them long I want to keep them, I want to let this sapling membership solidify and grow into a full grown tree.

Suddenly I feel a pang of panic. I am about to betray Eri's trust by Navigating her for information she has yet to give me. I am depriving her of the decision to entrust me with her innermost fears and insecurities. I am forcing memories out of her. The reason this group works is their commitment to honesty. They don't pretend to be alike or into the same things or to have the same strengths. They accept and tease lightly and laugh and enjoy one another. They trust one another. How would the group view what I am about to do? I know the answer. I'd say if they were to rate methods of trust violation, they'd place raiding someone's brain for information at the top of the list.

Chapter

17

I sit across from Eri in art class. She smiles at me as I sit down. She looks so at ease, so happy to see me. I have to remind myself that the end of our evening was awkward only for me. For Eri, it was just her sending me off with a compliment before shutting the door. *You're a good person, Leesie.* Am I?

Her calm smile, and maybe my own guilt, infuriates me. I hate when someone has it together when I am tense. The welling up and churning starts in my stomach and suddenly my face is hot. I take a deep breath.

I decide in that second to utilize my agitation as fuel for Navigation. As soon as I secure my balance on the stool at our table, I square my shoulders. I stare with flared nostrils and clenched jaw into her left eye. I feel myself collect like water in a filled sink when the drain is pulled. The spiral starts wide and slow. As it builds speed, it collects and tightens.

I am now inside myself, conscious of the split between body and mind. I can feel my body. I know that it sits across from Eri, stiff, and aside from the rise and fall of my chest, motionless. I have a connection to my body, but it's as if the plug has been pulled from the outlet just enough to prevent the charge from flowing. The two have only the smallest break in connection. But now my body sits, the idle plug. My mind, my brain, is the electric current in the outlet. Eri is the outlet. I collect, tighten, gain speed. I spin up inside myself. I can hear it, the spin. It's a tinny gurgle around my ears or somewhere in my head. The spiral narrows and narrows and spins faster and faster up into my face. I watch it surge up into my eye and then it's out. I black out as it, or I, travel out and into Eri's eye.

The dull burning begins immediately. But I adjust to the discomfort and focus on getting in and down. Immediately, though, I know this is different. I am in. I know that by the ache in my eyes. But I cannot See. I cannot make out a thing. I am in what I know to be her first layer, the layer of most recent memories. This isn't a layer that should be messy, gurgling, or sending obstacles my way. It's not a layer with answers or one that will house repressed memories. It's the easy outer layer, the couple of minutes to an hour ago layer. It's the tissue paper of the wrapping job to get through.

But this is dark. Thick. Like beef stew. Chunky and dense. I can make out globs in front of me. But I have no idea what the globs are, who they are, if they are memories or obstacles placed strategically in my way. The globs are cold and thick like pudding. I paw at them, half trying to get them out of my way and half trying to see if I can grab on to them to move them if I need to. My fingers sink in, but when I close my hand, the goo slips through my fingers the way the whites of an egg slip around the yolk. I am left only with an unexplainable ache in my hands.

This isn't right. She isn't right. *In the head.* She isn't right in the head? How can this be? She's Eri. She's normal. She has an above-average functioning brain that should be easily

Navigated. This is an easier Navigation than even the first mission Tobias sent me on. So where are the layers, then? Where are the usual finish line dividers that direct me deeper down? I don't even know which way is down. And why can't I See?

Despite the increasing burn I feel in my eyes, my thinking clears and I remember the Navigation where I had no idea which way was down. I had no idea where the layers divided. I couldn't See well. There were obstacles in my way. It was the missing-child Navigation. The aunt of the missing girl. The aunt I could barely Navigate. Because she was mentally ill.

I reach out instinctively to steady myself, forgetting that these chunky globs will offer me no support. I surge forward instead. Mentally ill? There is no way Eri is mentally ill. I would have known. Someone would have known, someone on the mission at least. Tobias? He would have been privy to that kind of information. There would have been signs, right? She can't be. A sudden panic surges through me as I imagine the worst. What if no one knows? What if I am finding it out right now?

As I careen toward hulking globs and churning gray and brown swirls, I know that my thoughts are swirling just as fast. Am I finding the answer? Is this the key to Eri's inability to excel at the pace her dad has set? Is it because she lacks the wherewithal to achieve because of something wrong with her brain?

The fear of this being true sends a sinking rush into my stomach like the sink you feel when you inch over the summit on a roller coaster to make that initial drop. That an-alarm-clock-is-going-off-in-my-stomach feeling jolts me. But quickly, the jolt fizzles. No way. Not true. Something is keeping me from believing that Eri is sick. But what? *I just know* is the only answer I come up with. I just know.

Eri's brain is not like the aunt's brain. It's not as cold. It's more gray, less brown. These globs . . . they're not attacking me. They don't have to. They're defensive. They're blocking, but not aggressively. It's like they know, this brain knows, Eri knows, that I can't get in. In the aunt's brain, I couldn't tell which way was down or where the layers were divided. It felt like the needle in a haystack cliché. I was searching for something that I knew was in there despite the challenge. But here I'm not searching. I'm walled in. I'm not in a hallway navigating through doors to find the answer. I am in a hall closet, closed off from not only the rooms that hold the answers but from the hallway itself.

So Eri's brain is not sick. But if she's not mentally ill, why can't I get in? And then it's there. The flutters and pangs of panic are replaced with a booming thud in the gut. I know why I cannot Navigate Eri. And I know it's not because something is keeping me from going in. No. Not something. *Someone.*

The only two scenarios in which a being cannot be easily Navigated, Tobias says, is if the being is mentally ill or if the being has been trained against Seers.

Trained against me? Eri has been trained against me? How does she know about me? About Seers? The thud in my gut turns into a wave of nausea as my mission explodes in my head. The burning in my eyes isn't unbearably dangerous yet, so I stay partly because I can't gather myself enough yet to get out and partly because I can't imagine, can't grasp, can't stomach, the fact that I have to face Eri in a matter of seconds.

She won't know I was in. They never do. Wait. I cannot expect the outcome of this Navigation to be like any other. She is not a "they." And all of a sudden I am faced with a new unknown. I think of the state the aunt was in at the end of my only guarded Navigation. If she had been aware that I was in her brain, she was in no state to articulate it. She was too busy shrieking at the realization that she had murdered her niece. And she was guarded because she was sick. But Eri? Eri's not sick. She's lucid. She's *trained*. I have to get out of here.

I take the leap. What else can I do? I have no answers anyway. I close my eyes and I am out. Instinctively my hands go to my eyes. No bleeding this time. Why would there be? I wasn't in long enough to do anything. I floated around in globs and went from mildly freaking out to full-fledged mania. Awesome.

"You okay, Leesie?"

Even with my hands over my eyes, I know. By the way she holds on to the *kay*, by the way she adds my name, by the way there is no real concern in her voice. She knows. I was in her brain and she knows.

"Yep. Fine. Thanks."

I take my hands from my face and drop them to the table. I have yet to raise my eyes to meet hers, and when I do I get what I expect. She's staring straight at me. I've been in full freak-out mode for what seems like forever, so I almost can't tighten up any more. But suddenly I don't feel so tense. I don't feel panicked or unsure or vulnerable. I drop my shoulders, pull my arms back, and rest my palms on the table. I can feel my stomach surging. I am not freaking out anymore. No. Now I am furious.

I hate when I feel backed into a corner. I have always understood why a caged animal will lash out and gnarl the hand that attempts to free it. At this moment I want to attack. I don't want to hear her side, not right now. Right now I want to run until I am far from any human, and I want to scream and pound the earth and throw things and let this sink in. I hate that I never have a moment. I hate that I always have to collect myself. I hate that I failed.

"Leesie?"

I ignore her.

"Leesie?"

No. Do not talk to me.

"Leesie!"

"What? *What, Eri?* What!" I spit the words at her. I imagine they are shards of glass. If she would leave me alone, give me a minute to compose, to figure this out, maybe I'd remember that I liked and trusted her a few minutes ago. But if she's going to jump right into an interrogation, fine. Bring it on. But this is going to hurt.

Her eyes narrow as she takes in my tone, the look on my face, the way I am poised with elbows bent, hands down, ready to pounce. Her hand goes in the air.

"Mrs. Tiller? Mrs. Tiller?" She's waving her hand now and turns in her seat toward our art teacher who is at the back of the room leaning over a sculpture on someone's table. "Mrs. Tiller!" The last urgent call pulls the woman up. "Leesie's, uh, sick. She says she's nauseous. May I walk her to the nurse? Please?"

Eri is stern and pleading, respectful and demanding. Mrs. Tiller is convinced.

"Yes, of course, dear. Please do. Take care of her, Eri. Feel better, Elise." Mrs. Tiller waves to the table next to ours to put away the supplies Eri had begun to set up. I guess she doesn't expect us back. Fine by me. I feign a weak and wounded wave and follow Eri out the door.

As she crosses the threshold and steps out into an empty corridor, I look down at my feet. My right foot is about to cross the same threshold. I will be alone with Eri in a matter of seconds. In a matter of seconds she will turn to face me. Will she speak first? Will she expect an explanation? Does she need one? If she has been trained to keep a Seer out, then she is aware that Seers exist. So I won't have to expose that, but does she know about the mission? Does she know about Tobias and my placement here? Has she known all along?

Before I am completely past the doorway, she speaks.

"Get your stuff. Walk immediately to my house. We will not speak until then."

I am taken by the tone of her voice. It's almost authoritative. She calls these words to me over her shoulder. She never turns around. She never slows nor quickens her pace. She doesn't turn left to E corridor, where our lockers are. She walks down the flight of stairs in front of her, towards the side door that exits to the staff parking lot. And she's gone.

Sweet, insecure Eri? Yeah, right. Ninja-brain, tells-me-what-to do Eri is more like it. All this time I was treading lightly, loving my place here, dreading a betrayal of Eri's trust. I was afraid to make a move, afraid to hurt her, afraid to Navigate her, and I was powerless against her all along? *Are you kidding me?* I do not like to lose, but what I hate more than anything is to be made to feel outplayed, defeated, and weak.

On the way to my locker, I make the conscious decision to shove everything that is in my arms now on the bottom shelf and grab only my wallet and keys. My focus on school is shot, so homework will not be an option anyway. Plus I need to go there with no baggage, nothing on my shoulders or in my arms. I need to feel ready for anything. After all, something tells me I will be meeting the real Eri in a matter of minutes, and I don't know what she is capable of.

Chapter

The walk to Eri's is quick. I force my brain to focus on passing cars, colors of houses, barking dogs, anything. It's when her house looms in front of me that I curse myself for not capitalizing on the precious minutes that have passed. I should have been strategizing on the walk over here. I could have been planning my opening should she leave it to me to talk first. It turns out I don't have to worry about that. She's at the side entrance door, waiting for me. She has one hand on the doorframe; the other holds the door open, beckoning me in. I study her face as I stride up the walkway. I try to decipher her expression. Is it one I have seen before on the face of the Eri I knew? Her eyes are narrowed, and her brow is creased. Her lips are in a straight line, but she doesn't appear angry. She definitely looks serious though, whatever her mood.

"Hurry up!" Eri calls in a clipped, curt tone.

I breathe in as much air as I can. I loathe being told what to do. She'd better watch it. I don't answer. I refuse to obey verbally or otherwise. As a matter of fact, I slow down a little. I never avert my eyes. I stare her down, attempting to let her know that I may not have gotten into her brain—she may have beaten me there—but I will not roll over. She has been given no title, no crown. This match is not over. She seems to sense my resistance. Her brow smoothes out a little. No smile, but she seems to soften.

I guess it would have been weird to lock eyes inches from each other as I brush by her into the house, but her staring straight ahead as I do is so cold. It leaves me feeling as if I am passing a stranger, an enemy, and it hurts me to think of Eri this way. I feel an instant pang in the gut as the possibility that I may lose her, or may have already lost her, bubbles to the surface. I continue to the counter to steady myself and will some of my fire back. I am better when I am angry. I am no good gooey and sensitive and worrying about friendship.

She shuts the door, and I hear her approaching. I do not turn. I do not look at her. No. You look at *my* back now.

"Leesie."

Her tone is calm. I have so many questions that I cannot bear to be stubborn. I cannot bear to ignore her. I pivot to face her. The air is thick between us, as if we're standing in a cloud.

"You're angry," she continues. "I'm not." She lets the words settle. She's looking into my eyes, into the space around my eyes.

Not sure what to say, I say nothing.

"I have been waiting for you to Navigate me. Now we can talk."

"What? You've been what?"

"I've been waiting for you to Navigate me."

Again she lets the words settle. She waits for me to gather my thoughts. It's as if she can see me wrapping my brain around what she has said. She knew I would Navigate her? How long has she been waiting? And why?

"You have been sent here on a mission to Navigate my father. My father puts too much pressure on me. It has been taking him away from his work. He is on the cusp of a breakthrough that will change the world of Seers. Getting me in order will enable Dr. Kuono to focus on that breakthrough. You weren't making enough headway. You decided to Navigate me for answers. You hoped the information you gathered from me would enable you to Navigate him sooner and more effectively. Is this an accurate description of your mission?"

Who is this and what has she done with Eri?

"Yes," I answer with as much authority as I can, considering I cannot feel my legs.

"Do you have any questions about this mission?"

She's leading me. I can feel it. But I have no idea where.

"Questions? What do you mean?"

"Is there anything about this mission that has you doubting its validity, its motive?"

"No."

"No?"

My mind is reeling. I rifle through the past twenty-four hours. Back in my apartment on my chair, I sat questioning my next move, my feelings for the group, and my feelings about the mission. What conclusion had I come to? Had I come to one? What questions had I asked myself? I couldn't reach them now. It was muddled like the cup of water used to clean paintbrushes. It was cloudy and an indescribable mix of colors inside my head.

"*I* am not the focus of this mission, Leesie."

"You're not the focus? What are you say—?" I don't bother to finish my question. It doesn't take a brain surgeon to connect the dots. She is telling me who the focus is by omitting herself.

I drop my eyes, nod once, and then raise them again to meet hers. "Why?"

"You know why. What haven't you been told?"

She doesn't need to say any more, and she knows it. It's always been there. That nagging question. That piece of doubt. Why all this trouble about the girl? Why the fuss over the daughter who seems to be doing okay despite the normal teenage self-doubt? Why Navigate the father to fix her? Unless I was meant to Navigate the father for a different purpose. Navigate the father who is working on a breakthrough that will change the world of Seers. A breakthrough I know nothing about.

It's true. She had never seemed broken enough. She seemed disgruntled, sure. But what teenager isn't disgruntled at some point? She has a family that loves her, an amazing group of friends. Besides, I was supposed to be moving into more challenging, more dangerous missions, Tobias had said. So why the human-interest story? Why all the fuss about a girl's feelings? A girl who happens to be the daughter of a neuroscientist. And a neuroscientist working on something that will change the world of Seers, at that.

I nod again. "So what haven't I been told?"

"You are not Navigating to help, Leesie. You are not Navigating for me, to make me a happier girl and my father a more focused worker. We've established that. You are Navigating my father to steal something from him to deliver into the hands of the Preceptors. You see, my father is not on the cusp of a breakthrough. That is just what you've been told. You are to know as little as possible about the real mission. The truth is, my father is desperately trying to keep safe the information you are trying to Extract."

She pauses. She's awfully good at allowing me to process information.

"My father was approached by a group of Preceptors over a year ago," she continues. "They exposed themselves as Seers and asked him to work for them. Naturally a neuroscientist who finds out that the brain is capable of far more than he could have ever dreamed jumped at the opportunity.

"My father began working with a brain, a Seer's brain, experimenting on the nature of the power of Navigation and Extraction. What he discovered, though, he soon realized cannot end up in the hands of Preceptors. Fortunately I was there to connect his memory of that discovery with a discovery about me."

Okay. Now she better pause.

"What? Back up. What discovery about you? Connected how? How do you know all this?"

"The day my father sat in his lab poring over months of testing was the day I told him what I am."

I don't bother to ask the obvious. I raise my eyebrows and wait.

"I am an Aurae. I read emotions, intentions, the way you read brains. Only I see it in colors. Hear it in waves."

"What?"

"Surely someone as smart as you didn't believe she was the only being with powers, the only possibility of it?"

"I had hoped, I guess."

This makes her laugh. "Yeah, I bet you did. That doesn't surprise me. Only Leesie is powerful. Right."

I am being mocked, and yet I love getting a glimpse of the Eri I know returning.

She goes on, "My father's memory of that day is linked to me because of the shock of his realizing the truth about powers of the brain, both the powers of Extracting and my power of Reading. They will not be a separate memory in that layer. You go into that moment to complete your mission and Extract, and you will have his motivation to protect me and the secret behind Extraction."

"And I was supposed to believe I was taking only the memory that leads him to overprotect you. I would have the Seers' secret without knowing I had it?"

I was catching up.

"Yes. And that information would have been taken from you."

"How? By whom?"

"By your Preceptor, Leesie."

I am so sick of the word *what*.

"What?"

"You are in danger."

Danger?

Being a Seer has always been a thing I could do. I used it to find things out, to help people, to help myself. Truth be told, sometimes I used it to amuse myself. I enjoyed playing around in people's heads, having an edge. I had never thought of it as something dangerous. Bleeding-eyes dangerous, yes. But that's just a physical drawback to the gift. She's not talking about that kind of danger, is she?

"The discovery my father has made, if placed in the wrong hands, could put all Seers in danger. You completing this mission successfully for your Preceptor puts you doubly in danger. Once they have what they want from you, your place in the world of Seers is questionable. You would be a liability. No one would want a connection to me or to my father to get in the way of the Seers' use of the discovery. In the worst-case scenario, you would be disposed of. In the best-case scenario? The memory loss would be extensive, and you have lost so much already."

"What do you know about my memory loss?" I spit the words out as fast as I can to stop her from going on to her next point. Does she know something about my past? Does she know why I cannot remember my life?

"I know that you have a very limited memory. And I know why. You are a valuable Seer. You not only go in; you also take out. Seers need you if they want to *possess* what is in someone's brain rather than just look at it. Think about it. You go in and Extract this information from my father, and it isn't his anymore. He doesn't know it, can't recall it. And only the Preceptors would have it.

They need you, rings in my ears. Right. I am more powerful than Seers. Because I am a Seer. And an Extractor. I never really thought of it that way.

"They needed you to need them," she goes on. "And you do need them if you have no one to rely on because you can't remember your life, if you need someone to put the pieces together for you, if you have no one else to turn to. Tobias was able to be that for you. He pretends to know what will make you stronger, what will help you regain your memory, if that's possible, so that he can send you on missions without question, so that you will work blindly for him, and so that you will trust him. But I have to tell you that I have reason to believe that it is Tobias who is responsible for your stolen memories."

This isn't the straw that breaks the camel's back. No. This camel is dead. Gone. Pulverized. I am spinning. Too many things are turning upside down. First she tells me Tobias would be stealing the information I Extract from Dr. Kuono and this mission has been a lie, and now she tells me that Tobias is the one behind my stolen memories? He's not only plotting against me now, but he has always been against me. Every meeting, every conversation, every piece of advice has been a part of his plot. Like fattening the veal calf for Easter dinner.

"Tobias?" These words escape like the last whistle of air from a deflating balloon.

"Leesie, I'm sorry. I've given you a lot to digest. I know this is hard for you—"

I interrupt her: "Hard for me? What do you know? Are you *Reading* me or something? Anything that was easy about my life must be in the parts I don't remember. I can deal with *hard*. What I'm having a difficult time dealing with is the fact that you are telling me to change everything. I have to change the way I see everyone. You, this mission, Seers, Preceptors, Tobias. He has taught me so much, given me a place to live, provided—"

"Provided what exactly? Mission after mission? Is it he who has given you so much, or is it you who have been working nonstop to learn at a rapid pace in order to be ready for this mission? Let me ask you, has he offered any explanation about your missing life? Your family?"

I can tell by the look on her face she is not asking me questions. She is proving her point. I meet her eyes.

"No. He says I just came to him one day. He's been trying to gather information on me—"

"That's a lie." Eri spits the words, half growling.

Her words hiss through the space between us and bite into the nagging part of me that doubted Tobias's explanations, or lack thereof, all along.

"How do you know? How can you be sure?" I half demand, half plead.

I need cold, hard facts now. If she is going to turn my life upside down, if she is going to talk me into doubting, challenging, rejecting my Preceptor—something that is just not done in the world of Seers—she is going to have to start producing evidence for her claims.

"The night my father discovered the secret behind Extraction, I went to see my dad at work. Something I never do. But this day was the day. I had decided to tell him about my being an Aurae.

"I developed the ability around eight. I aged into it, I guess. I have done some research, and there are a lot of us out there. Anyway, at first it was faint and slight, just a little color around someone's head if they were in a heightened emotional state. As I got older, it got stronger; the colors became brighter. I began to understand them and use them. I became lost in them for a while, distracted. I lost focus at school and in my activities. It caused a rift between my father and me. He is so success-driven, wants so much for me. So I couldn't wait any longer. I needed to tell him that day that I am an Aurae. That I was okay. That I was going to be everything he wanted me to be and more.

"When I walked into his lab, he was hunched over his papers with his head in his hands. He was nodding his head yes and shaking his head no at the same time. Next to him was a glass box, and it had something in it. Lights shone around it, and it was hooked up to electrodes. When I walked past it to stand in front of my dad, the box began to glow brighter. Green but mostly yellows. The rays floated and wafted out of the box and around my dad.

"In the box was the brain of a Seer. It was the brain my dad had used to conduct his research. The brain was hooked to electrodes and without a body to conceal my power to project color and possibly because of the electric current, I don't know, but it lit up the room. My dad could *see* the colors. Only Auraes see the colors of a person and can Read their aura. But this exposed brain was *lighting up the room*! Of course he freaked!

His specimen Seer brain was glowing! I immediately explained why and what I am. So for my father, the memory of the discovery and the memory of my being an Aurae are so close that they are one in that layer. This is the reason the Preceptors do not have the discovery yet. The memory is a jumbled mass they cannot clearly See. That's where you come in. Their hope is that an Extractor will be able to make it discernible."

"I had no idea that was possible, for memories to get stuck together," I say.

"Neither did I." She lets out a tired laugh. She stretches and steadies her eyes in front of her as she decides what to say next. I break in before she can continue.

"You keep saying 'secret behind Extraction.' And Tobias keeps saying Dr. Kuono's discovery that 'will change the world of Seers.' So what is it? What is this all about?"

Eri takes a step toward me, and we lock eyes.

"I don't know exactly, Leesie. My father won't tell me. He won't tell anyone. Anyone who knows the details behind his findings can be Navigated by a Seer and the information would be leaked. All I know is that his discovery is a formula. It's the key to what sets the brain of an Extractor apart from the brain of a Seer. With it, Preceptors will be able to transform Seers' brains. They will be able to *create* Extractors."

"Create Extractors? Why?" I weave my fingers into my hair, holding my head.

"Think about how much more power you have as an Extractor. Think about how different it is to view someone's memories versus stealing them. You could erase someone's memory. Someone's life. Now imagine Preceptors having the formula behind Extraction. Think of the power. And then think about it in the wrong hands."

"Oh."

"Yeah. Oh. Extraction is not a power all Seers should have."

"And what makes you this expert on Extraction?" I challenge.

"You are not the only Seer of your kind, despite what you have been led to believe," Eri responds quickly. "I know one and so do you."

Okay. This sounds like evidence.

"It's Luke."

As soon as the words leave her lips, I realize that I am not shocked, not even surprised. On the contrary, I find myself relieved. This explains his connection to Eri. And his connection with me. We share something in common that up to a second ago, I didn't think was possible to share with anyone. This changes things for me. Suddenly the fear of him faking a connection with me vanishes. Just the idea of discussing Extracting with someone who can do it overshadows anything else I feel right now. I feel validated, empowered, and less . . . alone.

"This makes you happy," Eri says as she peers at me. She sounds as if she's mulling this over. This may not have been the reaction she had been expecting. She continues to watch me. She seems to be looking around me, not into my face directly but into the space around me. *She's an Aurae*, I remind myself. She Reads in colors, Reads auras.

"What color am I?"

She smiles a little. "You're pumpkin orange floating in a sea of purple."

"Is that good?"

"For you? Yes." Eri chuckles again at my expense.

"What is that supposed to mean?" I lean forward, frowning. When did I become so hilarious to her?

She laughs again. "You're on fire, Leesie. All the time. Most people are blues and greens when they're calm. Your calm is a cooled-off red, sometimes a pale orange, but I've never seen you green. You are always somewhere between contained rage and moderate annoyance. It amuses me. I think it's because you try so hard to feign an air of collected nonchalance."

I hate knowing that there's no point in denying my moods to her. Color rushes to my cheeks as I think of all the times I must have pretended not to care or be annoyed by something, and she knew I was secretly bubbling.

"So I run hot. Got it. And what's the purple?"

She smiles again, a sly, slow smile. "Purple is content, blissful, enamored, passionate," she says.

Eri locks eyes with me. She knows. And by the look on her face, I believe she wants me to say it.

"Oh." I look down.

"Oh?"

"What?" I shrug and look off past her.

"What do you mean 'what'? Leesie, you know I can *Read* you. I have been Reading you since you got here. I know how you feel about him."

"That's news, considering I still haven't figured it out."

She smiles again. It's good to see her smiling. I have to wonder if she feels like she can relax, let loose around me a little, now that I know what she is. But this makes me realize how many more questions I have.

"Tell me about being an Aurae."

She settles into her position at the counter. She leans toward me, shifts her weight from one foot to the other, tilts her head to the side, and starts: "I see people's faces, bodies, gestures, as you do. But then I see around them. Everyone projects colors that signify mood and general disposition. Greens and blues, I told you, are calm, relaxed colors. Purples are passions. Reds are frustrations, anger. Yellow signifies fear, distrust. Shades in between allow for the mixing of moods and emotions. I see shades as well: whites and blacks."

She pauses and searches me, checking for understanding. She had me until the whole "shades" business. She senses my confusion.

"People shade themselves if they are in a state where potential action trumps emotion. They will look like they have thrown a sheet over themselves. This happens usually when they are 'ready to pounce,' so to speak. The motivation behind their actions shields any color from showing through. All I can tell then is whether their actions are motivated by positive or negative force, if they are good or bad. Like you when you were trying to Navigate me."

Crap. I knew this was going to come up. I knew she would demand an explanation as to why I felt it okay to violate her trust and violate her brain.

"And?"

"You don't have to ask me, Leesie. You know why you did it. I know why you did it. I know you were trying to help me, help your Preceptor, and help the mission. I know you care about me."

Her words rush me in a warm gust. I lean on the counter to steady myself. I am shocked by the amount of relief her words bring.

"I have known since you got here that you would find your way to the truth of this mission. That you would choose sides. You have chosen sides, haven't you?"

My gut tells me I have. My gut has always told me, I guess. All those questions, all those times it didn't feel right. And this group feeling like friends, like family. But . . .

"But what does that mean, Eri? What does choosing sides mean?"

"It means a new mission. It means us. Us fighting to keep critical information from landing in the wrong hands, in the hands of dangerous Preceptors. Us. You, me, my father, and Luke . . . against Tobias and everyone working with him."

I was already on a side until a few minutes ago, and that's been working out so well. . . .

As much as I think I trust Eri and Luke, I can't help but wonder if I am jumping out of the path of an oncoming car by crossing into another lane of traffic instead of heading for the safety of the side of the road. The question is, who's on the side of the road waiting for me? No one. So I join them. Otherwise, I'm alone.

Chapter

Eri had taken my nod to mean I was in. My head was moving in allegiance to her before my brain could catch up. My heart was in it before I could think it all through. I guess I have known for a while now whose side I was on.

What's funny is, now that I think back, I wonder what was at the base of my loyalty to Tobias. I was puppeting what is expected of Seers, I suppose. I was given my expectations and guidelines and was blindly obeying. "Here is your Preceptor, Elise Felton. Here is your life from now on, Elise Felton." And I opened my arms and took it. What else was I supposed to do? But I search myself for real feelings of gratefulness or affection for Tobias or the few other Seers I have met at the Philadelphia headquarters. I have none. All business.

Add to that what Eri tells of the Preceptors in charge, of Tobias. He has been sending me on missions to evaluate my skills. He has been calculating my strengths to gauge if I am ready to Navigate for what he really wants. He has been using me.

And he is responsible for wiping out my memories. But how? He can't Extract. Can he? Now that I know Luke is an Extractor, the door is wide open as to how many of them exist. If Tobias cannot Extract, maybe he sent someone after me who could.

That one hurts. Using me because I am valuable? Seems feasible if you are a power-hungry freak, which apparently he is, but stealing my life? How cold, how heartless, how evil, is that? Have I been missed by loved ones? Do they watch the news, read the papers, and post flyers, holding on to some remote possibility that I am out there somewhere? Did I have brothers, sisters? A best friend? A boyfriend? I don't know at the moment which is more painful: the fact that my memory loss could be devastating lives or the fact that I have been willingly working for the man who has devastated mine.

I kick a stone off the sidewalk as I move swiftly down Delaware Avenue. Away from Eri's. Away from Alsinboro Academy. In the other direction. Away from the center of Preston toward the outskirts and into a neighborhood I've never bothered to traverse.

I needed a minute. I needed some air. Eri was calling Luke. She was asking him to come over right away. She wanted us to discuss things further. She wanted me to hear Luke's side, she had said. He has details to provide me with. Details about his mission. Details about his plan. That makes sense, but clearing my head takes precedence over anything else. So here I am. Walking alone and going nowhere. I know that in a few minutes I have to turn around and head back. There is no avoiding the next step. And I don't want to avoid anything. In fact the more I stew, the angrier I become. I am intimidated, yes, by the idea of going after my Preceptor, but I know I'm "red," as Eri says. I know I run hot. I know I will not shy away from the opportunity to fight back. But Tobias has always seemed so smart. He always seems to have all the answers and to know what to say to focus me or correct me. I have to get used to thinking of him as a liar. I have to get used to the idea of having to try to beat him at a game he says he's only begun to teach me.

In front of me at the end of a tree-lined street is a house the color of an avocado. It has mango-colored shutters and stained glass in the front door. A herringbone-patterned brick walkway directs my eyes from the sidewalk to the front porch. I continue my gaze up to the second-story windows, where I can make out the wispy lines of lace curtains. Up the roofline, left of the chimney, sits a rooster atop an arrow. This weathervane, its bright copper hidden under a pale green film of patina, turns slightly to the right as the wind picks up. I stare at it as it mocks me, and then I laugh out loud at the irony of this bird. Yeah, rooster, I see you. I'm turning. I'm turning.

And I do.

As always my brain is in overload. When I should be reeling from all I have found out today, I end up thinking about nothing or noticing everything or, like now, taking in the architecture. I shake my head, determined to focus.

Luke is an Extractor like me. With that information comes a new plan. Luke's mission that will somehow protect Dr. Kuono's information *and* take out Tobias. A mission that according to Eri cannot be completed without me. Fighting with them means I get more time with them. I let this possibility plant roots. I let myself get excited. It seems too good to be true that I will continue to have this group on my side as my friends and as close to a family as I have. Whether they think that strongly of me is irrelevant, considering they have other people in their lives that care about them outside this group of friends. I do not. These feelings were bubbling under a closed lid before this afternoon. Now I get to take the lid off the pot and leave the water boiling rapidly. The steam can escape and cloud my future with possibilities of listening, lounging, laughing, loving. . . .

My stomach flips and pings as if there's a beginner band student in there beating the mess out of a triangle and calling it music. Because he will be there. I will see him in a moment. And he will talk to me. Really talk to me. *Confide* in me. The perplexing nature of our connection is now replaced by the inevitability of it. The depth of it. Eri telling me someone is like me, and not just anyone—*Luke*. This changes everything. She took the jokers from the deck. Now we're playing cards.

In front of her house, I look for Luke's car. It's not parked out front. It's not in the driveway. He's had enough time to get here from school. Where is he? I am too amped up for idle time. Where else does he have to be that's more important than this? I hope he doesn't think I'll sit around and twiddle my fingers waiting for him to show up on his prized steed. I'll go get my own horse. I can feel the frustration frothing in my stomach like it's capping off a cappuccino.

Before I reach full-fledged flip-out mode, I see him. In the doorway. Watching the street. Watching me. He must have walked, or run. He is waiting for me. *Good. That's more like it.*

I slow my pace a little. The triangle resumes play in my stomach, and I can feel my cheeks flush red. I cross from sidewalk to slate conscious of my feet. I am watching them land from one stone to another as I make my way to the door. Why? Why am I watching my feet? I hate that. It's a sign of blatant insecurity, weakness. I have to get a grip. I force my eyes up and am glad to see he has moved away from the door. *All that for nothing. He's not even watching me walk up here.*

Luke must have gone to tell Eri I am back, because now she is at the door, holding it open for me like before, only she holds my gaze this time as I enter. She smiles easily. She seems relaxed, as if she had no doubt that I would return.

"Have a nice walk?" she asks teasingly, as I make my way to what has become my spot at the kitchen counter.

"I did." I scan the room for Luke. Wherever he is, he is not in the kitchen.

Making a grand entrance, are we, Luke?

"He went to the study to grab something. He'll be right back."

What, is there a color for 'Where's Luke?' now?

I don't bother to play it off like I wasn't actually thinking that. I hate that she not only assumes she knows what I am feeling, but she has the nerve to be right, too.

I must have gone fire-engine red because she quickly adds, "He's grabbing my father's files. They'll provide you with information leading up to the discovery."

"Leesie."

I turn to my right to see him entering through the dining room.

"I hear you've had a busy day."

Does he have to toy with me and get me all riled up right off the bat?

"And I hear you're quite the powerhouse."

"No more than you."

And in a few strides he is within three feet of me. His mouth is relaxed and smirking, but his eyes are serious. He wants to start light, I guess, but it is clear that the purpose for our meeting will outweigh any niceties or flirtations.

Eri cuts in: "Yes. Great. You're both great, overachieving Extractors at their best. Seriously, you guys can do this later. We have a lot to discuss before Leesie needs another walk." She shoves Luke and shoots me a look.

"Hey! Really? All you threw at me and all I needed was a walk? I think that's pretty remarkable actually."

"Speaking of which," Luke says, "Eri filled me in on what you know so far. We have a little more to throw."

Okay. I guess small talk is over.

I lean in and listen as Luke fills me in on how he came to know about the Preceptors' plot to coerce Dr. Kuono into discovering the secret to creating Extractors.

I only got distracted by the curve of his bottom lip once and the shape of his jaw a couple of times. Not too bad.

Luke starts by giving me information about his own background. He has been in Preston for a few months. He came to Alsinboro Academy for the same reason I did: to get to Eri. Before that he had been with his Preceptor since the age of three.

I remember back to what Tobias told me about Seers finding their Preceptors. Three is the youngest known age for a Seer to venture out seeking his mentor. The younger the Seer connects, the stronger the Seer. Seers that strong go on to be Preceptors themselves.

I try to imagine Luke as a Preceptor. He is definitely leadership quality. He commands respect, gets attention, is listened to. But he isn't cold and demanding. Is he? The Luke I have seen interacting with his friends, and even the Luke who has softened with me at times, seems more protective and nurturing than possessive and imposing. Maybe Preceptors just become that way over time.

When Luke gets to his ability to Extract, my mind stops wandering and I redirect. He says he hadn't realized he possessed a special set of skills that other Seers do not until the age of eight. He doesn't give me the details. I'm not sure if he does this to save time because he has so much to tell me that certain details must be cut or if he is not ready for me to know all the specifics. I am sure of one thing; I can tell by his tone and the fact that he does not stop for clarification that interjecting with questions would be frowned upon. I'll just have to hope that I have the opportunity to ask him later. The story of his first Extraction is at the top of my list of things I want to know.

He must have had a relatively contented childhood, because up to this point Luke has been relaxed and matter-of-fact. Tobias once explained to me that in best-case scenarios Preceptors and parents work well together. They form a co-parenting bond for the good of the child. Sometimes not. Sometimes parents reject their "gifted" child and the Preceptor takes over. Tobias comforted me in the loss of my family by telling me it was likely I would have lost them anyway. I should have turned against him then. . . .

From Luke's telling it sounds like his Preceptor took charge of him but that his parents kept in contact. As Luke moves into the years following his first Extraction, a cloud comes over him. It's not a glooming, dragging cloud. It's a black, dry force that promises not tears of rain but destructive sparks and booms.

He arches his back and sets his shoulders, and as he continues I learn that Luke's views are ones that I didn't know existed. Views on the way Seers operate. Particularly the Preceptors.

I listen as Luke explains through tight lips that some time ago, because they already filled a leadership role through mentoring young Seers, Preceptors decided to join regionally and work to organize and manage area Seers. Their goal was to ensure that enough training was completed. This training became known as missions.

At first missions were completed for training purposes only. Soon, though, additional missions were assigned by need. Since Seers are part of general society, they overhear problems at every turn that could be helped by Navigation. This could be overwhelming, even distressing, to a Seer. Seers could end up resenting or hoarding their gift so as not to feel exploited. To avoid this, to avoid animosity, to avoid overexposure, Preceptors took on more of an administrative role.

Previously Preceptors had been only mentors to new Seers, but they grew to form regional governments reining over all Seers in their designated areas and assigning all missions. As their power increased, so did their interest in Extraction. After all, Seers are in charge because they are the most powerful. So when the Seers they have mentored since early childhood suddenly displayed an ability to Extract, the power card exchanged hands. And since Preceptors like their role as kings of the Seers kingdom, they set out to do something about controlling who becomes Extractors. If they can ensure that Preceptors and all their minions become Extractors, they can ensure that their power remains intact.

"They took the power, and then changed the game. They changed why we See. They called it a 'mission,' and suddenly we work for someone. But who? General society? No. The good of humanity? No. We certainly don't work for ourselves. So we end up working for them. The Preceptors. And now they want to make sure we keep working for them. They can't stand that some of us age into Extractors and that if we don't want to, we don't have to follow them anymore. Only we've been taught to follow them, to look up to them, to think of them as family. And does the worker challenge the boss when the boss is *family*? Do you see the problem?"

Suddenly his eyes are earnest.

I lean back and straighten up. "Yes. I see."

That's not good enough for him.

"Tell me. Tell me what you see." Now it's his turn to lean forward. He rests his arms in front of his chest. He's bent over at the waist, and with me upright, we are even-eyed as I search his. He seems to have a lot resting on my answer.

"We have been blinded by the blurred lines. Preceptors are revered elders, fathers to us. We must not challenge or question. So, as they quietly slipped into power, we barely noticed. And anyone who did knew better than to question it. Our powers are being controlled, and we are either accepting of it or unaware it's even happening," I say softly. I am careful to meet his piercing gaze as I complete my last sentence. Luke raises his eyebrows slightly. Something flickers in his eyes. Something you see in a dog's eyes when he's gotten out. The dog stops in front of his owner as she calls him. For a second she thinks he will wag his tail and happily obey, following her back to the safety of the yard. But instead he pounds his front paws, lowers his head, and after the telltale look, he bounds off in the opposite direction. Why do I get the feeling Luke is ready to lead me away from the safety of the yard and toward a busy intersection?

Finally he nods slightly and says, "Good. Now we begin."

"Begin what?" I ask, confused. Aren't we already in the middle of something here?

"You need to understand why this power structure was created. Preceptors went from mentors to manipulators and you need to know why," he says. "Have you ever wondered why, since you found your Preceptor, you have been handed mission after mission?" He waves an arm in the space around him as he addresses me, "Are you asked if you approve of the information you are retrieving? Are you even given all the necessary information about those missions? At what point was it accepted that Preceptors would decide how much or how little the rest of us know? And who? Who gave them the authority with which they rule? Did I? Did you?"

As Eri walks over and reaches out to touch Luke's arm, hoping to reel him back in, I realize I am leaning so far forward my chest nearly touches my arms resting on the counter. I'm drawn in not only by his words but by his passion. I had no idea he would sound so informed, so enraged, so powerful. I had no idea he would make so much sense.

I don't have the years of experience with a Preceptor that Luke has. But two things I know for sure. One: Seers are definitely not given all necessary information before they are sent on a mission. I am present proof of that. And two: Seers are not free to Navigate as they see fit. Once you connect with your Preceptor, there is no such thing as Navigating for pleasure. And if there is, no Seer ever mentions it.

I have Navigated for pleasure or for no reason at all. Sometimes I go into a being's brain simply because I can. That person may be particularly aggravating, and I decide it's a way to avoid prolonging the interaction. Since I have been with Tobias, I have done this a couple of times. The secretary at Alsinboro comes to mind. I was agitated that day. She was annoying and condescending, so in I went. Not for any real purpose, just to find out what makes her tick. To find information I could turn around on her. To have her eating out of my hand by the end of the meeting. Which I do believe she was. But I never told Tobias.

What's interesting is I don't remember ever making a conscious decision that if I were to ever veer from the carefully laid-out path of Seeing before me, the path Tobias set, and Navigate someone on my own, I would not tell him. But I had. At some point I decided not to tell him. Something inside me told me not to. And I had no plans of telling Tobias about my attempt to Navigate Eri. As a matter of fact I had a feeling of anxiety every time I thought of his finding out.

As I listen to Luke's passion, his conviction, I wonder if I would have ever become as angry as he is if I had never had the opportunity to listen to him now. Would I have been smart enough or an independent enough thinker to challenge the system as Luke is? I don't consider myself a runs-with-the-crowd person. But it feels so natural to follow him. I know part of it must be my infatuation with him, but the other part is that he is hitting on so many points of contention for me. I have had so many doubts. So many things about the world of Seeing have seemed senseless or unfair. I have had so many questions. I have had no one to talk to. No family. No friends. No other Seers like me.

I listen to him now, going on at Eri's prompting into the way he came to know about her, her father, and her father's discovery, but all I can think about is how lonely he must have been, distrusting his Preceptor in a world where trusting one's Preceptor is paramount.

Focus.

It seems that as Luke began to doubt his Preceptor he also began his life as a spy. He began gathering information not only against his Preceptor but against all regional Seers in the Delaware Valley, which includes Central and South Jersey, Philadelphia and its suburbs, and southern Delaware. His covert operations exposed the plot to Navigate and Extract Dr. Kuono's discovery.

"Tell me more about the Preceptors' motivation behind controlling the creation of Extractors," I interrupt as he pauses his speech and paces back toward me. "If they just want to level out the playing field, if they just want to ensure that they, too, have the power to Extract, shouldn't it stop there? Eri said *danger*. Tell me the danger."

Luke doesn't seem bothered or even surprised by my redirection. He seems to feel the need, though, to stop his pacing, plant himself a foot from me, and look me in the eyes in order to let me know that what he is about to tell me is anything but good.

"Dr. Kuono possesses the formula of Extraction. The formula completes a sequence that will fill in a gap in Seers' brains. Once applied, the Preceptors in possession of the formula will be Extractors."

"Right. I get that. But—"

He shakes his head.

"The danger lies in the secrecy of this. This is not a mission cleared by the Seers organization. The group of Preceptors involved in this mission believes that only they and the doctor know about this. Their mission is to send an Extractor in to take out the memory so that only they will possess the secret. Dr. Kuono will no longer possess the memory. It will be Extracted from you. Only these Preceptors will have the knowledge that the formula of Extraction was ever sought after much less found."

This last thought he utters seems to trigger a spark in him. His nostrils flare and he grinds his teeth as I watch the muscles in his jaw flex.

His eyes pierce me as he almost whispers, "Know this. Once you have this secret, they will not rest until it is taken from you."

His agitation only works to fire me up. "Great. So they all just want to, *what*? Dance the Irish jig in my head? Have a party in there? Awesome. And what aren't you telling me?"

He pauses to clear his throat. "Dr. Kuono's findings are in the hands of Preceptors already because he was working for them. It was the Preceptors who provided him with the brain Eri told you about earlier, who gave him the mission, who started all of this."

I raise my hand to object, but Luke was expecting that. He shakes his head at me again and continues.

"Dr. Kuono was excited, floored by the possibility of it all. You don't have to try very hard to convince a neuroscientist that the brain is the ultimate in untapped power. When he was faced with the reality, with proof, that brains were capable of so much more than anyone is aware of, he was in. Dr. Kuono knew he was working for Seers on a breakthrough and on the possibility of making Seers into Extractors. But he did *not* know their intentions."

"How did he find out their intentions? He did find out, didn't he? I mean, that's why we're here talking about this like we can intercept the discovery, right?" My interruption has the slightest twinge of panic to it, which I hear and hate instantly. Too many questions. And the answers aren't coming fast enough.

"I told him."

Well, that answer was quick.

"You?"

"You find that surprising?"

"That you're working alone? Just you? Against the Preceptors? Yes. A little."

"I am not alone, but our intentions are to continue to expand the army, so to speak," he says with just a touch of suggestive flirtatiousness. I'd love to reciprocate, but the timing couldn't be worse. I decide to bypass that road and conduct business as usual, but not before I slip in a slow blink and little half smile.

"An army against Preceptors? Why? Tell me what the Preceptors intend to do."

"Preceptors are planning to use this information to imbed the ability to Extract in all chosen Seers. Extractions would be done at the command of Preceptors."

"Uh, okay . . ." I trail off intentionally to let him know I am still not buying all the hype.

"Leesie, you don't see the danger because it has never occurred to you to Extract for other than helpful purposes, right?"

Other than helpful purposes? Like what? My mind begins reeling like a movie scene that follows its actors on a roller-coaster ride. As I tick to the top, gaining height and gaining momentum, I begin to piece together what this means. I begin to see, for the first time, Extraction as a weapon. What could I do with it? I begin to see memories moved to recessed layers. Something that happened last week I could grab and drag down to a third-year layer, where memories just sit but cannot be recalled. That memory would be essentially lost.

What kinds of memories could I move? Memories of successes, failures. People? Could I erase people? And what if I Extract memories all together? What if I take them out with me? What if I take layers out? Couldn't I change who people know, what they can do, what they are capable of? Could that be what was done to me?

By the time I steady myself and meet Luke's stare, my roller coaster has pulled back into the station. I have been down one horrific dip after another. I am even nauseous, as I would be if I had actually ridden one.

And I know what he means by danger.

If the Preceptors use Extraction as a weapon, they will destroy people's brains. And quite easily, too. No one would even know.

"Everything we talked about earlier, about Preceptors starting as mentors and now being our bosses, points to this. *They* want to be able to control who Extracts. They want to safeguard *their* number of Extractors. So that a rise of rebel Extractors can never overtake them."

"And once they have all that power? What then?" I shudder as I ask.

"I'm still working on that one, Leesie." He raises his eyebrows a little as his eyes search mine.

"All right, Luke. You're right. Danger. What do you need me to do?"

Chapter

I walk toward Alsinboro, toward my truck, feeling heavy. I feel tired from being tense all day. I don't know how many hours my shoulders have been hunched up or how many hours my nostrils have been flared, but I swear even my face is tired. I have to suck it up. I have reading to do. I have journaling to do. Luke and I are just getting started.

He walks next to me, saying nothing. He seems to need a break from talking, and I am happy to give him one. We were at Eri's for nearly three hours before we got to this point, the point of me having enough background information for us to make a plan of action.

Now we walk back to the academy to part ways. I go home to digest and read, and he goes home to do more of his super-spy work, I guess. As much as I look forward to being alone in a short while, I can't help but to feel uneasy when I think of going to my apartment. My apartment that sits atop the regional Preceptors' headquarters, atop Tobias's offices.

How is it for him? I wonder. I mean, he's using me, right? I am just a girl with a special power on a special mission. As long as I report to him and seem to be doing what I am supposed to be doing, he doesn't care about anything else. He shouldn't watch my comings and goings with vested interest. Then why won't Luke come back to my apartment with me? I hadn't asked him, but he addressed it when it was decided that I would take the files back home to read them and familiarize myself with the particulars of the discovery. He said he would come to answer any questions and to discuss the mission further, but that it wasn't wise. *Wasn't wise.* What does that mean? Is Tobias onto Luke? Or is it me? Am I being watched? Could Tobias suspect something? Or could Tobias be watching me already simply because of how important this mission is?

Alsinboro beckons ahead of us now. We cross the street and turn left toward the parking lot. His car is close, but he doesn't lose stride. He must be walking me to my truck. A few feet from it, he slows and turns to me.

"You holding up okay?" he asks lightly.

"Sure. Fine." I try to sound light, too, but there's a heaviness I know we both can hear.

"I know it's a lot, Leesie. I know what it's like to lose a Preceptor. It sucks."

Luke does know what I am feeling, and I take comfort in that. I hate when people try to fit their negative scenarios into yours when they offer words of understanding or encouragement. They usually come off sounding weak or just plain stupid. As if they're trying to compete or don't get it at all. Luke's not trying to make me feel better. He seems to know that I will be okay, or at least he is leaving it up to me to figure out if I will or not. I hate when people say "hang in there" or "get over it and move on." I wish people knew that telling someone what to do with their own emotions usually does not go over well. . . .

"Yep. Sucks," is all I reply.

I don't have it in me at the moment to be coy or clever. Oddly enough, I am alone with him and I don't feel like flirting.

He moves a step closer to me. "Look, I know we're not done here. I wish I could stand here with you all night. I wish we could forget about Preceptors and missions for a while and concentrate on *other things*. But we have a lot to do. I'm not blowing you off. We just both need the night to figure things out. I'll talk to you tomorrow?"

Wow.

Blunt. Direct. Explains himself without prompting. Plans time for me in the near future. And then proceeds to clue me in as to exactly when that near future is. What's he got the manual that gives step-by-step directions on how to deal with me? I'd pinch myself, but I don't believe in self-inflicted pain for the sake of a boy.

I refrain from swooning and pretend I'm not fazed by his care and candor so that I can test him to see if it's an all-the-time behavior or something he's just throwing at me now because we are in the beginning stages of whatever this is and he's on his best behavior. You never know.

"Sure. Tomorrow's fine. Bye, Luke."

I make brief eye contact, just long enough for him to say, "Bye." Then I look away and walk on to my truck. No lingering like a needy dog. There's nothing worse than a dog that begs and circles and stares immediately *after* getting a treat. You want to make a mental note not to offer a treat again until it learns not to appear so pathetic. Get the treat and move on. Have some self-respect.

It surprises me that I can focus on my fluttery feelings for Luke on a day when my powers of Navigation and Extraction were thwarted, my friend Eri is actually an Aurae—something I didn't even know existed until today—and my mission was exposed as a plot to potentially turn Extraction into a mind-erasing weapon. But I'm glad I feel fluttery—it's a distraction, and a pleasant one at that.

The pleasant distraction doesn't last once I'm in my truck. The realization that I am going home and that Tobias will inevitably summon me is unnerving. I know in a second that I cannot go back. Not yet. I need something to fuel me first. I reach for my phone and dial Daisy's number.

"Hello?" It's evident in her voice that she's surprised I'm calling.

"Daisy. Hi. It's Leesie."

"Leesie, hey. Everything okay?"

"Sure. Um, I'm sorry to bother you. I know it's dinnertime, but—"

"No. No bother. You feeling okay? Frances said you left early with Eri."

Leaving art class early seems like a lifetime ago, considering all I have learned since then. I rush to explain: "Right. Weird thing. Must have been my lunch. Something wasn't sitting right. I went to Eri's. I feel okay now."

"Oh. Good."

"Look, Daisy. I realized today that I lost a bracelet. I think I may have dropped it at the stables. Do you think it's all right if I go there to look for it? Would I be allowed in?"

After assuring me she'll text me the address, call ahead to the barn to prep them for my arrival, and telling me she hopes I feel better and that I find what I am looking for, we hang up.

I hope I find what I am looking for, too, Daisy.

Saanen Stables is alive with activity when I pull into the parking area next to the barn. In the riding ring is an older woman on a black horse. She's addressing three young riders. Jumps are set up around them. The barn light is on. I pass a boy in chaps with a bridle draped over his shoulders and a western saddle in his arms. He nods to acknowledge me as he leaves the barn. Once I'm inside I realize I am alone.

I pass Jackson, who is nibbling hay, and Mr. Fellerman, who is whittling away at the wood of his stall, and I inhale deeply as I make my way down the row. Is she in here? My footsteps inspire curiosity. Heads poke out of stalls on both sides of me. And then I see the dark chocolate brown of Cleo's noble head.

I stop in front of her, and she regards me the same way she did before. I send my breath out across her nose. She pricks her ears. I rub the velvet of her lower lip. She nips the collar of my shirt. I slide my hands over her jaws. I will the familiarity of her touch and her smell to take me somewhere. I close my eyes.

Nothing happens at first, but as I settle in, regulate my breathing, and remind myself of the connection I felt when I was last here, a scene begins to play in my head. It's jumbled and charcoal gray, but I know that I am inside a dark building. I am sitting on something cushiony like sawdust or straw. I am holding a wriggling object in my arms, and another, much larger, object looms over the top of me. I run my hands from

Cleo's face to her neck, and I lean into her as she moves her head to the side, letting me hug her. I melt into her warmth and into the feel of her. I press my eyes tighter together. And I know. The wriggling object in my arms is a foal. I am in its mother's stall. She stands over me calmly as her baby's lanky limbs surround me, its side and belly warm my lap, and its fuzzy head rests on my shoulder.

The scene is a small piece, so it cannot fill the gaping holes in my head on its own. But it's a start. Allowing this barn and Cleo to alert my senses enabled me to remember. I *remember* something. Tobias may be lying to me about a lot of things. But it turns out he was right on about one thing. I am getting stronger.

On the drive home, I drown myself in music. I turn up the volume as loud as I can stomach and constantly change stations, replacing every song with one faster than the last. I need drums crashing, screaming lyrics, and preferably songs with themes of power or vengeance. After two dumb love songs and one about accepting oneself, I give up and turn off the radio. I roll down the windows all the way and push on the gas a little more instead. I don't want to lose this feeling. I hadn't known whether my memories were repressed or removed. And I still don't. I cannot account for all of them. But I can say I got one back today. And I have a plan to see about getting back another.

On the way up to my apartment, I think about tomorrow and about Luke and Eri's plans for the very near future. Eri's plan centers on taking time to strategize. She seems content with the fact that we are all on the same page now. We have no more secrets, so of course we can fight this. I just don't think Eri's is operating at a high enough speed. Preceptors are one mission away from having the ability to control Seers becoming Extractors. And then they control Extractions. We're talking life-alteringly dangerous. For Seers. For Eri, too. For Luke. For Dr. Kuono. Daisy. Patrick. Frances. They are all involved, and they are all expendable. Eri's plan of waiting and working together doesn't sit well with me, knowing that the lives of all the people I care about are on the line.

And Luke's plan? Luke's plan that I'm not privy to? I think it's because he isn't done hashing one out. Or maybe he's got to clear it with his army. At Eri's he put an emphasis on getting all the background information before we develop a plan of action. So I was to come here tonight to read through the files. But knowing that we need to intercept the knowledge of the discovery from Dr. Kuono so that it never ends up in the hands of Preceptors, isn't that enough in order for us to move forward on this? There isn't much time to discuss or decide. All this wait-and-see nonsense is for the birds.

I perch in my chair and stare out at the cityscape. I am waiting for something else. I don't have to wait long.

"Good evening, Elise."

"Hello, Daniel."

"Ready?"

Daniel is accustomed to waiting patiently in the doorway for me as I gather my things. But tonight I grab nothing.

"Yes. I'm ready."

When Tobias spins to address me seconds after I've settled in my seat, his eyes fall to the clear desk pad in front of him.

"Forget something, did you?"

"No. I haven't written yet today. I wasn't well."

"Not well?"

"No."

I try to focus on his questions. They are always fast-pitched, and he expects readied and complete answers. I have never fought such a battle with my body or with my face before. The battle over my body is easier. I have commanded it not to lurch forward and unleash a pounding complete with torn flesh, biting, and kicking. And I can't attack him anyway, not before I get some answers. I am tuned into the level of tension I'm displaying in my shoulders and hands. But the tension in my face. How am I doing there? It's agonizing to mask fear and loathing and instead display respect and reverence.

"I see. And you have nothing for me, then?"

"I do."

"Oh?"

"Yes. When I had a bout of nausea, it was Eri who got me out of class. I spent the afternoon at her house. She let me rest and gave me something for my stomach. I made headway with her today. I am sure I'll be invited over to her house after school tomorrow. And I don't see why I wouldn't be permitted to stay until her father gets home."

"And you are ready for Dr. Kuono? You know what memory you will Extract?"

Tobias seems to be trying hard to keep his body and face

relaxed, too. And he's doing a decent job. Too bad the veins popping out of each temple are giving him away.

Now is the time. I slide both of my hands from my lap to my stomach and take a deep breath. I stand suddenly. I rest both hands, palms down, on the desk pad in front of me. I continue to lean forward until I am almost assuming push-up position. My face is inches from his. I inhale as deeply as I can. I pinch my eyes closed.

"Elise! What is this?"

I take one more breath and let myself go. I've taken Tobias by surprise enough that he is frozen. I take advantage of the stillness in front of me and lean in. Just a little closer. I feel him suck in air. He shifts back slightly.

"I'm sorry, Tobias. I apologize. My stomach. Something still isn't right," I sputter. I stand up straighter but clutch my stomach with both hands.

His look of disgust turns to one of horror. He must be picturing the effect vomit would have on the cleanliness of his desk.

"Go. Go! But I expect an entry. Tomorrow. Now, go!"

I'll go. I'm done here, anyway.

Chapter

On my previous missions Tobias has always supplied background information. Addresses, phone numbers, physical descriptions, information about family dynamics. Having this information enabled me to Navigate or to Extract successfully.

But I have been left to my own devices when it comes to *my* background. I have been given no addresses, no phone numbers, and no physical descriptions of loved ones or family members, much less any information about the nature of my lost family dynamics.

Where are the files on me? Surely the extensive research conducted daily at headquarters on strangers, strangers we meet for missions and then hear nothing more about, pales in comparison to the amount of research that was conducted on me, a fellow Seer. A valuable Extractor.

But to my own devices I am left. And on my own devices I rely. And on my own senses. I spend the rest of my evening pouring through the files on Dr. Kuono and sifting through my own head.

Thanks to Saanen Stables I can now see a horse. A roan mare with a white stripe from forelock to muzzle. She half walks, half trots to me as I enter the paddock. She bypasses my waiting hands and nudges my pocket where she knows she will find an apple, always an apple. She knows me. She knows me because she is mine.

And thanks to the musk, the heavy, spicy perfume I inhaled as I leaned in close to Tobias, I can also see a row of houses, brownstones, with marble front steps and elaborate wrought-iron railings defining each front porch. A cement retaining wall separates the sidewalk from the properties, which sit back from the street. They are towering and formidable. In the center house, the one with no blooming marigolds, no mums, no shrubbery or manicured lawn, in the center house, in the center of the doorway, behind the full-glass storm door, stands a man. I know him. I know him because he is Tobias. Tobias exists in my memory. My old memories. *Before I showed up at his door.*

When I finally go to sleep, I feel resolved. Empowered. I'm ready to challenge the system, fight with Luke and Eri beside me. I feel like a genius with an ingenious plan.

But when I wake up in the morning, I feel like a naked tree. Because today I will be shedding my leaves and blowing my cover to Tobias.

I am not going to say anything. I am going to hand Tobias my journal and watch him read it. What will he do when he reads about my memory of him? What will he do when he realizes I *remember* things at all? What will he do when he realizes I know he existed in my life before it was taken from me and that he can no longer pretend he had nothing to do with it? Will he squirm in his seat? Will he gasp in shock? No, not Tobias. It will be subtle, a sight change in expression. But if it is as Luke and Eri believe, if he is the one who stole my memories, he *will* react, and I will know.

Both Eri and Luke are in the parking lot when I finally arrive. They have exasperated looks on their faces, as if they are sick of waiting or worrying.

She's at my window before I can put the truck in park.

"You're late! We have almost no time before class! Where have you been?"

"Doing my nails and putting together this fabulous ensemble. You like?" I make sure my words have a slight snarl to them to top off the sarcasm. *Like I would be late intentionally today. Right. I'm an idiot. Give me more credit than that, Eri.* I step out of my truck, slam the door, and add, "I was in traffic. Philly, remember?"

"Oh. Sorry. You don't need to get all red on me. I was worried."

When was I going to get used to this *Aurae* thing? I use a little sarcastic attitude to convey my annoyance and hide my anger, but she can see the whole thing in color.

"I know. I should have called or texted or something. Just an accident on the bridge. I didn't mean to make you worry." She watches the air around me as I speak, and a smile starts and spreads. I don't even think she listened to me just now. I guess my colors are more interesting to her than my words.

We turn and head a couple of parking spots over to where Luke stayed when Eri ran to interrogate me. I'm guessing he knew it wouldn't go over well.

"Traffic?" he asks.

"Traffic."

"I tried to tell her. But she was imagining one horrible thing after another that could have happened to you." His eyes search mine. Then I watch those dark eyes dance over my face, my hair, and pause at my lips.

He's watching my mouth as I answer, "And you? Not worried?"

"No. I don't worry about you."

Such a loaded statement. How does he manage to speak volumes in a single sentence? Is he saying what I think he's saying? I need to be sure.

"Good," I answer, being sure to remove any tone, any inflection, from my voice.

"Yes. It is good."

So he *is* saying what I think he's saying. He doesn't worry about me because he doesn't have to. Well, that's a relief. With all that overprotective hovering he does with Eri, I was concerned that he was just that way. He was just one of those guys who cares about a girl and turns into Super Boyfriend, flying around, saving her from other boys, herself, the world. Gross. I wouldn't be able to tolerate that. I can't be coddled. I can't be cajoled or cooed at. I need to *just be*. And I want a guy to *just be* with me. If he keeps this up, he just may get the job.

I guess I have to make sure I live past today so that can happen.

We would have continued to stare at each other at least a couple seconds longer, but clearly Eri has an agenda.

"Leesie, did you read the files? Luke, are you ready to tell us your plan?"

As I nod yes Luke begins to tell us.

"We need to Navigate your father today, Eri. We'll meet at your house. I have been going over and over how we are going to do this. How we can Extract the information and keep it safest for the longest amount of time. We need time to find out how deep this thing goes, how many Seers and Preceptors are involved, how many enemies we are going to have. Leesie will go in and Extract the memory from your father. And then I will go in and Extract the memory from Leesie. That will buy us some time. Tobias and the others will not expect the information to be in my brain instead of hers." Now he turns to me. "You will continue to report your progress to Tobias. Give as much information as you feel will suppress him. You will tell him you need more time—"

"No," I say. I wasn't going to tell him what I plan to do when I meet with Tobias today. But now I can't help but tell. His plan has me buying time with Tobias. I will live above Tobias, answer to Tobias, report to Tobias. No. If he took my memories to send me on this mission, if he took my life, stripped me of my past and my identity, my family, then no, I will not continue this relationship past today. His rule over me ends today.

"What do you mean, no?"

"I mean, *no*. That's not how this thing is going to go. It's going to have to go my way. According to my plan. And you're not going to like it."

His face seethes with frustration. His mouth turns down in anger. But his eyes. His eyes dance in my fire.

"I agree that we should Navigate and Extract Dr. Kuono

today. I'm not crazy about the idea of you Navigating and Extracting me, but it does make sense. And it will buy us time. But as far as my meeting? I have some breakthrough memories. I remember a few things from my past. They play in my head like movie previews."

"You're going to tell him that? That you're remembering? What's that going to do? That will do nothing but possibly get him thinking he should mess with your memories again. He'll just monitor you more closely. It'll make next week that much harder."

"Leesie, Luke's right," Eri cuts in. "You don't want to evoke any suspicions."

"I'm not finished." I clip my words razor sharp at the ends. How can I get them to see my side if I can't present them with the whole scenario? "I am not interested in just giving him information about the return of a few memories. I am interested in providing him with information concerning one memory in particular. I have a scene that plays in my head of me on a sidewalk somewhere in the city. I am facing a stretch of row houses. I am staring at the door of one of the houses, at the man in the doorway. The man is Tobias. I am sure of it now. It hadn't meant anything to me before, but now . . . if he is responsible for taking my memories and I tell him that I remember that day—"

Luke interrupts: "It'll be as if you're telling him you remember everything. Even though you don't. You tell him that and he will think you know everything. How he intercepted you, what happened to your memories, everything."

It's quiet for a second as we all process.

"So you're ending this today, then. You do this, you challenge him like this, accuse him like this, and you will have to leave immediately. You will Navigate Dr. Kuono and go," Luke says finally.

Why is he surprised? Of course I am ending this! Or starting this, depending on how you look at it. I have to. I have to get to my life. A real one. And I have to remind Tobias and myself of what I am. The more powerful one. He has toyed with me. He has stolen from me. And yet I have worked for him. My gut burns and I feel as if I could rip flesh from his face if he were here. That I could squeeze it and let it ooze between my fingers. That I could stare at the gaping raw-meat wound where part of his cheek used to be and smile.

And I will not meet with him and make nice. I will not stand before him, reporting to him as I have done in the past. All the times I listened to him, took his advice: "Tobias says this" and "Tobias says that." I have been violated, and I am ashamed that I let him get away with it for so long. That I didn't figure it out on my own. So I will tell him about my memories. I will remind him who the powerful one is. He may have outsmarted me, but in the end I have the better brain.

"I know what the accusation will do. I will present him my journal, a journal I use to provide him with information about my missions. He will read about the memory I have of him. And that will do it. Yes, I am ending his false sense of reality in which I am a memory-free moron and he is in charge. How can I continue to meet with Tobias now that I know what he has done to me?"

"You can't." Eri, who has been silently watching, now commands our attention. She was Reading us as we spoke. I can tell. She has that look on her face. The one she wears once she has figured me out and wants to tell me all about myself.

Instead she turns to Luke. "I don't want her to go either, Luke. But having her here another week. One more week? What's that going to do? This setup is ending. I liked it, too. I liked my new friend. She listened to me and spent time getting to know who I really am. Mission or not. She cares about me, and I care about her. I don't want to lose her either."

Eri turns to me now. When she leans in for a hug, I worry that it could be weird because I haven't known her long and we've never touched before. But it isn't. It's like I am hugging someone I've hugged a thousand times before.

When we break our embrace, Luke steps toward us both and rests his hand on Eri's shoulder.

"You're not just losing Leesie, Eri. I'm going with her."

Chapter 22

"Eri, look at me," I say, gripping her shoulders. She wipes the tears from her cheeks and sniffs a few times. "Eri, you may lose us, but let's think about this. It won't be forever. We'll handle this. We'll stop Tobias. And we'll get every other Preceptor involved. This isn't a permanent good-bye. I promise. It's not."

I don't know if that's something I can promise, considering I just ensured her that Luke and I will be blowing the top off the abuse of power in the world of Seers and Preceptors. That's quite a promise. But why can't we? Why stop with Tobias?

She's Reading me. "Okay" is all she says. She's not stupid. She knows it's a tall order. I'm sure she Reads that I am unsure, but I hope she also Reads that I am determined. I am not lying to her. I may not be able to guarantee victory. I can guarantee that we will do everything in our powers to end this and get back.

"I can't go in, Leesie. I can't just go to class now," she whimpers.

"We have to," I insist. "Don't raise any suspicions. Anyone could be watching, right?"

"Right. Great. Awesome."

"Careful, Eri. With the attitude. You're starting to sound like me."

I put my arm around her and turn her toward the front doors. She puts her head on my shoulder for a second and then straightens up. She pulls her shoulders back and clears her throat.

That's right, Eri. Suck it up. It's going to be all right.

We float through the day, slightly aware of things, slightly outside of ourselves. I see Eri and Luke walking together to class. I wonder what he said to her. I wonder if he apologized or explained himself. What is his explanation to her? I'm sorry to leave, but I am choosing her, not you? It must feel that way to her, even though he is choosing the mission and the fight against Preceptors and trying to keep her, her father, and her friends safe in the process. But it will sting the sting of rejection nonetheless.

I both look forward to and dread going to lunch. I want to see Daisy and Patrick and Frances. But it will be hard to see them. I miss them already.

"Looking good, Leesie!" says Patrick. "But what's the matter? You look distracted. Did you see your reflection in the dining-hall window and get yourself all flustered again? You gotta stop taking your own breath away, girl. I told you about that."

He's priceless. Can't I figure a way to bottle him and take him with me? Life is just better with him in it.

"Very funny. I'm fine. Tired maybe."

"All three of you look tired. Where was the party? You look like you were up all night."

We sidestep the unwanted attention. Each of us starts a conversation. Eri turns to Frances, I ask Daisy how Jackson is, and she eagerly inquires about my bracelet and about how I'm feeling. Luke gets Patrick going by bringing up how his training for the next race is going. We try to pep up. But a heaviness surrounds us that we can't shake. I am willing the clock forward despite cherishing these last moments as a group. The next period is art. My last art class with Eri.

Just yesterday I sat across from her and attempted to Navigate her. Today I sit across from her and see an Aurae, a friend, and someone I will miss terribly.

She leaves her canvas in front of her to grab paint and brushes from the back of the room. She has been working on this piece the past few days. I stand up and walk around our table to face it. It's Boathouse Row at night. The white string lights on the houses dapple the purplish black sky. Her blending of colors is elegant. I guess she would be good with color.

"You like?" she says, trying to imitate my voice when I used those sarcastic words on her earlier.

I laugh. "Yes. I do. It's beautiful."

We get to work. Me on my sketch of horse and rider and her on the finishing touches of Boathouse Row. We are both immortalizing memories. Trying to hold on as long as we can. The silence is relaxing. It's not until the bell sounds that I realize that the school day is done. And that means my meeting is just around the corner.

"You're going to be okay, aren't you? Luke may not worry about you, but I can't help it. You don't know what Tobias is capable of. What if he takes your exposure of these memories as an accusation? What if he retaliates?" Eri's voice is pinched and shaky.

"He *will* take it as an accusation, because I am accusing him, Eri. He is responsible for my missing memories. He is responsible for messing with you and your father. Let's not forget the things we are speculating he will do once he has the ability to Extract. He'll do it. All the things we talked about. Changing people's lives, destroying people. He'll do it. He is capable of it. I'm going after him."

I'm cooking up to something here. I can feel the rage in me moving and churning. I need this. I need to be fired up before I get home and lose my nerve. "I'm taking him down. For what he did. For what he's going to do."

"Aren't you scared? Haven't you thought about the fact that you have to get out of there? You're planning to drop this bomb on him and then, what? Say, 'Okay Tobias, nice talking to you. Bye'?"

"I'll figure that out once I'm in there. I'll be fine. Just go to your house. Wait for me there. I'll be there by five. *I will.*"

"Okay," she answers. She Reads me one last time and goes.

Luke is at my truck. Of course.

"Hey," he starts.

"Hey."

"You ready?"

"I'm ready," I say flatly, even though I want to follow it with a question: You don't think you're coming, do you? But I wait.

"I think I should follow you," he says. "Look. I'm not trying to invade your space. I'm not trying to protect you. I just want to be there in case."

"In case what?"

"In case you don't come out."

Well, I can't argue with that, can I? For Eri's sake, for Dr.

Kuono's sake, for the sake of all Seers and Extractors, I have to come out. And if I don't, Luke needs to hightail it to Eri's to protect her and her father.

But I am going to come out.

I think he will read the journal entry. I think he will look at me with raised eyebrows that will deepen the crevices on his forehead into caverns. He will ask me about the memory. He will ask for specifics. I will be vague and toy with him. He won't like it. He will ask about the mission. I'll be vague again. He'll want to explode, but he won't. Tobias is calculating, methodical, exacting. He researches and waits, waits and researches. He will not be ready for a rash move. He will dismiss me and immediately begin plotting retaliation.

And I will be a move ahead. At Eri's. With the information he wants planted safely in Luke's brain.

"You can follow me because it makes sense. And it will help Eri to not freak out as much. But I am going to come out." I finish with raised eyebrows that challenge him, dare him to disagree with me.

He sees my challenge, and it seems to amuse him.

"I know," he says, "but I want to be there when you do."

He had been leaning on my truck, a favorite pastime of his, but now he stands straight and takes a step forward. His eyes never shift from mine, but he moves swiftly. His arm is around my waist before I can react. I don't move my feet an inch, but my body curls back as I inhale sharply. If we were dancing, this would be the point at which I dip. Instead I straighten up and tilt my head back.

We've been entranced so many times. So caught up in each other so many times. That this first touch, this first embrace, should feel awkward. But one fits in to the other like a puzzle piece finding its place. Our faces are inches apart, *too many inches apart.*

I melt into him for a second before my arm curls under his and slides around his back, and I pull him closer. He sighs deeply and puts his other arm around me. He has been waiting for this, too.

In a swirl of minutes that could be hours or seconds, we lose ourselves as our lips do the dancing while our bodies are still. In this moment there is no mission. No discovery. No danger. *Well, there's danger. But this danger is fun.*

As if a bell sounded, we release each other. Time's up, and we know it.

Now the difficulty is trying to focus after that.

"Okay, then. I guess I'll have the air on the whole way there," I say as I fan myself and bite my lip.

He laughs. It's the loudest and best laugh I have heard from him. He puts a hand on my shoulder to steady himself while the laugh dwindles to a chuckle. He eats it up. The compliment. Everybody wants to hear they can get someone all hot and bothered.

"Right. I'll open my windows, too," he says, and laughs again.

And we part. That's how we leave it. It's perfect. No heaviness. No warnings or rehashing of plans. Just a kiss . . . and a laugh.

Chapter

As soon as I turn onto Girard Avenue, I lose Luke. He has purposely slowed down, and I'm assuming he'll circle around and park after me so we don't pull up at the same time.

It had taken me until I was over the bridge to get focused. If this mission were me conducting research on Luke's kissing style, there'd be no problem. Since it's not, I had to get a grip and remember what we're doing here. This is a big deal. I park, take a deep breath, and get out. I focus straight ahead on the door that leads to the stairway up to my apartment. I don't want to look around and accidently see Tobias in a window, or any Seer, for that matter. I don't want to be beckoned into his office before I can get to my apartment to get my journal.

I unlock and open my door and turn immediately to the left. I had set my journal there on the table last night. But now there is nothing on the table but the little brass tray I use as a key holder. Where is it?

I jerk my head up and cross the room to my desk in the corner by the kitchen doorway. Maybe I just thought I set it on the table for easy access. That's it. I just forgot.

The desk is clear. I snap my head to the right. My chair is empty except for a throw pillow. I bound across the room and jerk up the cushion. Nothing.

A bomb goes off in my chest. Because I know what this

means. I know what happened. Tobias doesn't like to be kept waiting. And he wanted that journal entry. So he sent Daniel in here to get it.

Crap!

What am I going to do? He's downstairs! With who knows how many Seers. I'm a sitting duck. Every once in a while, the cocky overconfidence I feel before doing something turns out to have been blatant denial. This is one of those times. How could I have thought Tobias would have been that easy to play?

I take a breath to collect myself. He'll let me come to him, won't he? I'll walk in, and he'll be sitting, waiting with the journal in his hands. He'll relish the look of surprise and panic on my face. And then he'll have me surrounded.

So I'll walk down as if I'm heading into his office but just keep going. I'll just leave. Yes. I have to leave. *Now.*

I cross back to the door. I look at my hand to make sure I have my keys, and with the other hand I turn the doorknob.

Just before I open the door, I listen. I should hear quiet. It's just me up here. Just my apartment at the top of a landing. I am the only one who uses this stairwell.

Then why do I hear the slight tapping of feet on the stairs?

Do I? Am I just being paranoid?

No. I hear them.

Definitely feet. Definitely coming this way.

My body begins to react without bothering to confer with my brain. Suddenly I am across the room again, through the kitchen to the chair by my window. I am up, standing on the cushion. I shove my palms on the glass of the window and heave up. The old window creaks and groans, and the wooden frame splinters as it slams open. I dig my fingers into the metal lift handles to raise the screen. The screen is old, like the rest of this place, so it sticks and resists my efforts.

With the screen three-quarters of the way up, I make myself as scrunched as possible. I ease both legs out, put my weight on the back of my chair, and flip over so I go out butt first. I want my feet to hit the fire escape while I'm still grasping something, so I can see if the thing's even sturdy enough for me. I also want to watch the door as I exit.

The fire escape wobbles under me a little, but it's all I've got. No going back in now. In fact I'm sure I see the door handle turning as I drop onto the landing. When I attempt to stand and take in my surroundings, it occurs to me that Tobias could have sent people out here, out back, to be sure I am coming down. Or he could have someone at my truck. Once again, no going back now. I make my way down the grate steps to the next landing. I look to my right down the alley. I can see Girard. My best bet is bolting and hoping I see Luke's car. My feet plant solidly on the cement, and I poise to take off. I hesitate and decide that bolting seems predictable. And conspicuous. If I take off, I'll stand out on the sidewalk, which an hour before rush hour is only slightly peppered with people. I decide to hide myself as much as I can and hug the sides of the buildings on the way to the street as I look for Luke.

Thanking the weather channel for telling me it would be a chilly day, I tuck my conspicuous hair down my back into the hooded sweatshirt I put on this morning. I guess a girl with a hood covering her head is conspicuous, too, but it's not as much of a bull's-eye as my mass of curls.

I hit the sidewalk and back up to my building. I glide against the bricks to the corner, climb over a gnarled mass of rust and wire, which was once an intact fence between the neighbors and us. I hug the neighbor's building. The scary truth is that if they are looking for me, they will see me. I feel a little hidden, though, just by not being in the middle of the sidewalk. At the corner of this building, I am out of hugging options. The next structure is not a house, but a church. Its back is gated with that kind of black fencing that look like rows of arrows joining hands and pointing to the sky.

With no buildings left to shield me, I make a break for it. At the corner of the house, I turn to face Girard and take off. I convince myself that I can make it. Until at the corner of Girard, I see three men by my truck. One is in front of the driver-side door. He is tall and lanky. He watches the front entrance of my building. Another is in front of the passenger-side door. This man is younger but bigger than the other two. He is scanning the sidewalks up and down Girard. The third is standing in the street directly in front of the truck itself. He blocks my truck's path as if saying, *You'll have to run over me first.* He is burly and nasty and looking in my direction.

The panic and fear I was feeling is instantly smothered. In its place is a sickening rage that I can feel travel through me. And suddenly I don't want to hide. I don't want to run. I want to rip their faces off. How dare they? How dare Tobias? What have I done to him, to these punk followers who have my truck surrounded? How do they plan to stop me? Hit me? Attack me? I wish I could rip out the fire hydrant I am about to run past and beat the three of them to a pulp with it. Other than that I see no other object I can grab that will sufficiently batter them beyond recognition.

But at once I recognize something else. Luke's car. He is inching slowly onto Girard. He must have been circling the block. I don't know whether I am relieved or disappointed. Three grown men, against me? I would have gone down. But I would have gone down swinging.

As soon as Luke sees me, he stops the car, and I rush into the street to jump in. Just before I close the door, I glance behind me at my truck. The man in front is gesturing toward me, pointing and waving the other men forward.

But I am in. They don't have a chance.

Of course, now they have my truck. *Awesome.*

"Are you okay? What happened in there?" Luke blusters.

"I'm okay," I say, trying to catch my breath. "He knows. Tobias knows," I quickly add as I turn in my seat to watch the men behind us. They are rushing into headquarters. No one seems to be jumping into a vehicle to follow us, though.

"He sent someone into my apartment. He sent someone to get my journal."

"It was gone?"

"Yes," I say, letting a twinge of defeat creep into my voice. I hated to hear it, but I knew I felt it. I was supposed to be a step ahead, not Tobias. He's been ahead this whole time, toying with me and using me. I feel so dumb, so duped. And now he has duped me again.

"He was sending you a message."

"Yes."

Luke takes his eyes from the road for a second to look me over. Checking me for injuries, at first, but then he looks into my eyes. I bet he wishes he could Read me like Eri right now. Although he always seems to read me in his own way.

We're on the bridge in no time. I call Eri and tell her to scrap the original timeline and be ready in fifteen minutes. We are no longer waiting at her house for Dr. Kuono to come home. We are picking her up, and we are going to his lab. Now.

Chapter

24

The rest of the ride to Eri's is a blur of talking and fast driving. I fill Luke in on my narrow escape. We are barely in the driveway when Eri catapults down her front steps. I swear she's in the backseat before the car comes to a stop. And we're off again.

Thankfully Luke fills her in. I'm sick of the story already. I'm ready for this to be done. To be done with Tobias.

"My father is expecting us," she adds once she's caught up.

"You told him?" I ask.

"Yes. He knows the plan. He has known. It was his idea to wait for you to be ready to join us. I wanted to tell you right away. As soon as you got here. Luke had already told my father and me that you were coming and what your intentions were."

"Right."

I keep forgetting that Luke has had months with her. He came here and laid the groundwork for their friendship, gained her trust. Then he told her about his mission and the Preceptors' plans for her father. And he told Arashi Kuono and got him on board. Then they waited for me. That thought ignites me. Why? Why did they need me?

"Luke, why did you wait for me?" I demand.

"What? What do you mean?" he asks quickly.

"You waited for me to get here. For me to get here to Navigate Dr. Kuono. Why? Why didn't you just do it? Why didn't you go in and get the information yourself? If you can Extract, why didn't *you* do it?"

He shifts in his seat. He speeds up a little. He moves out of the right lane to pass the car in front of us.

"You haven't told her?" Eri's words aren't accusatory. They're surprised, disappointed.

"No. I haven't."

And then silence.

"Do I have to ask the obvious, Luke, or are you going to start talking?" I demand.

He sighs, readjusts his grip on the wheel, and starts: "I already tried. An Extraction. I wasn't able to retrieve the memory. I couldn't do it. It's big, Leesie. Two memories in one, and he's so smart. The obstacles are bigger. The layers are thicker—"

Already tried?

"So what makes you think I can do it?" I snarl.

"I've been underground in my investigations. I have been under the radar and gathering as much intelligence as I can. And from what I have researched and from what I have heard, you are the strongest Seer, the most advanced Extractor, anyone has ever seen. That's why Tobias came to you. He doesn't need *an* Extractor, because remember, I told you before that there are others. He needs *you*."

"I'm so great, huh? Why was he able to get my memories, then? How did he do that?" I spit the words at them both. Such a backhanded compliment. You're the best, Leesie. Fabulous at taking things *out*. Oh, but you can't keep anything *in* to save your life.

Luke winces a little. Maybe at the fury in my voice or maybe because I am getting closer to the reason he hasn't told me the whole story until now.

He feels sorry for me. Ugh. The thought of his pity makes me sick.

"We don't know," he admits.

Or maybe because he doesn't know.

No one knows how Tobias was able to erase my memories. That must mean no one knows if I have any chance of ever getting all of them back. I think of the few memories I have creeping around in my brain. Is this spell, this curse, whatever it is Tobias has done, wearing off? Or did he just miss those?

Eri attempts to soothe me: "Leesie, I know your memories are an important part of your fight against Tobias, but we need to focus on Extraction right now. For my father's sake. For the sake of everyone involved."

Of course she's right. And I haven't thought of her enough. Her *father* is in danger, and I am worrying about myself.

I refocus and readjust my tone when I address Luke again: "You said I should go in and get the memory and then you'll Navigate me to throw Tobias off the trail. But if you can't get the information from Dr. Kuono, what makes you think you can Extract it from me?"

"It's a gamble. I'm not sure. But the research Dr. Kuono has done since seems to suggest that his memory of Eri being an

Aurae and his memory of the secret of Extraction will separate once they're in your brain. If that's true, I should be able to Extract just the memory of the discovery."

For the rest of the drive, we wear silence like a blanket we're using to shield us from one another.

"No pressure, right?" I say as we pull into a space in the parking lot of the research facility where Dr. Kuono works.

They say nothing. I'm glad. I am not in the mood for anyone to cop an attitude with me. I am the only one allowed to do that right now. They seem to know better. In fact, we don't speak. Not a word. At the front desk. In the elevator. Down the creepy corridor to the last door on the left. Nothing.

Good. They're smart enough to shut up.

Eri grips the doorknob and begins to turn it. Luke is poised and ready to step in right after her. I am behind them, smirking and secretly pleased with myself at having been able to scare them into silence.

But then . . .

We're all scared.

In the lab, behind the table, sits Dr. Kuono. Next to him, behind the brain, sits Tobias.

Chapter

I am behind my two allies, realizing that makes them my shields. I can't let them shield me. I don't know what Tobias intends to do to us, but I know he views only Dr. Kuono and me as necessary to this equation. I leap forward, squeezing between Luke and Eri, and thrust my arm across Eri's chest, sending her stumbling back.

"Leesie, no! Dad! Are you okay? Dad!"

"Honey! I'm okay. I'm sorry. I didn't know he was here! I shouldn't have told you to come—"

"I beg to differ, Doctor. Our guests have arrived on time." Tobias hisses his words, and they float heavily in the air like smoke rings.

"Elise, I'm afraid I've changed the locale of our meeting. Will this suit you? We have so much to discuss. You've been keeping so much from me."

Luke huffs next to me and lurches forward.

"As you were, son. My fight is not with you. Not yet." Tobias mocks Luke and then refocuses on me. "Do tell me. How much do you remember?"

I'm not sure whether it is fear or fury that has my tongue held captive. I don't know if I am able to string words together to form an answer.

But I have to. I have to answer him. And I have to face him—

for Dr. Kuono, who was misled; for Eri, who is blameless in all this; for Luke, who's fighting to protect us all; and for myself. If I want my life, I have to face him. I don't deserve my own life if I can't.

"I remember *you*."

"Oh? And what of me, Elise?"

"I know." I stammer at first, but I swallow and inhale and continue. "I know, Tobias. You were there. In my old life. Why? Why did you do this to me?"

I feel like a ventriloquist dummy. But instead of one person lending me his voice, I've got two. And the tone is a blend of quipped and quivery and vicious and venomous. One of them has got to go.

I step toward Tobias. I glance at Luke, who is watching me. I say again loudly and more deeply, "Why did you do this to me?"

"How could I?" he mocks. "I am no *Extractor*."

"You son of a—!" Luke lunges for Tobias again.

I go with him this time because my left hand is around his upper arm as I attempt to keep him from launching himself across the table into the brain and onto Tobias. When Luke feels me charge with him, he stops. His heavy breathing is almost a snarl, but he holds back his bite.

"Elise," Tobias responds coolly. "You must housebreak your henchman."

"What do you want? *What do you want?*" I bellow.

"You know what I want by now. I want the Extraction formula. And I am going to get it."

"Never."

"No?" he sings. "Are you sure? How can you be sure when you don't know what your decision will cost you?"

"What do you mean *cost* me?" I spit.

"I'm no Extractor. Not yet. But I have several under my charge. You know that Eri, even with her exceptional skill set, has no defense against Extraction. And the dear doctor here. And even Luke. He may have offenses, but he possesses no defense. And the others. Daisy, Patrick, Frances. They are so young, so full of promise. To lose them would be such a shame. To see their identities stripped from them, their memories erased. Well, how would you forgive yourself?"

"Don't listen to him, Leesie!" Luke thunders. "You can't just think about us! Think about how many more people are in danger if he can Extract!"

"Don't let him win, Leesie!" Eri calls.

Tobias raises his hand to quiet them. "It's not just them, Elise. You want your life, too, don't you? Don't you want your precious memories back? If something happens to me, well, you will never know the life you had."

Tobias is covering all his bases. His words drive me down. Like a nail under a hammer, I sink. How can I win? If I don't Extract for him, everyone I have met on this mission will lose their memories, their lives as they know it. If I take him out, I will never get my life back.

In a flash I think of Patrick's perfect smile, Daisy poised on her horse, and the way Frances looked at the lunch table when she helped us understand the math test. Her brain has so much to offer. The thought of her or any of them losing even the smallest part of themselves is too excruciating to bear. Eri. I see her across from me in art, smiling easily. I see her swaying behind her cello. And Luke. I see part of my future when I see Luke. I can't let anything happen to them. I know what I have to do.

"No! You will not hurt them. You've already hurt me. But not now. Not anymore. I'm stronger than you, Tobias."

I cannot tell Luke or Eri what to do next. I have to hope that they know their job is to take care of Tobias and secure this room so that I can Navigate Dr. Kuono. *Now.*

Eri moves forward. She doesn't say a word. Luke fixes his eyes on her and shifts to the side as she approaches the table. They move like synchronized swimmers. Fluid but furious. Eri watches her father. She seems to be telling him something, or maybe he is telling her something. And then I know. She is Reading him. She nods ever so slightly to no one in particular. To herself. She has an idea. She turns her head away from her father and fixes a determined gaze on a new being. The brain. Directly in front of Tobias, she stands erect, strong, brave. She refuses to look at him. She refuses to acknowledge him. She must feel what I feel—that we must be swift. Our actions must be exact and must be first. Tobias is not to be given the opportunity to act.

Even before she reaches her hands out, the brain begins to glow. But when her hands touch the glass box, the glow becomes a gleaming beam of moving light. There's a razor edge to the beams that makes it impossible to see. It's as if we are standing at a swimming pool's edge and the glaring sun that dances on the moving water both stings and confuses. We are spinning in a glowing kaleidoscope. I squint and stumble a little to the left. Instinctively my hands go to my face.

Instinctively. Of course! That means Tobias is squinting now, too, right? His hands are in front of his face. He's distracted. She's distracting him for me. I can make out Luke. He puts his hands on Eri's shoulders and shifts her farther to the right as he takes his place beside her directly in front of Tobias. That's the last thing I see before I step up to the table, lock eyes with Dr. Kuono, and go in.

I am already prepared for the worst. But I realize I am not prepared for this.

I am used to obstacles, but these are not coming at me. I am surrounded by them. I cannot swim down and into layers here. The surging, swimming-with-the-current feeling I am used to is replaced by the feeling of standing in the ocean attempting to jump the waves, only the ocean is angry and fierce, and even the sand is against me. It keeps sliding away from my feet. At the same time the waves come at me like a prize fighter charging, gloved hand raised, and swinging a right that can knock me out of the ring.

The only thing I have to go on now is the fact that Luke has been in here. And he didn't succeed. I will need to do something he did not do. I think of Luke. He would fight this. He would identify the challenge and he would flail and trudge against it. And that didn't work.

I let my legs go limp. I make myself smaller, straighter. Like licking a thread before sliding it through a sewing needle, I will try to make myself long and slip through. I put my arms against my ears, press my fingers together, and attempt to slither like an eel. I feel less resistance already.

I travel down through cold clumps. The ooze thickens to grayish brown sludge. I go down a little further, and the clumps now have the consistency of clay. It's getting harder to move down. I feel like I am shoveling through rocks.

I take a second to think. I have to remember who I am in. This is a sane, decent, intelligent man. His brain should not be intentionally trying to fight me. I remember what Luke said about the memory being big. Everything around me is big, thick, gooey, which tells me I am where I need to be. It's thick because I am in the right spot. This is it. This is the double-memory that I need. That should be it, but there is a hulking problem. I am in a mass. How do I know what to grab? What is here to Extract?

I try to focus. It's like looking through glasses that are an inch thick. I can See movements and blurred images. It's mostly gray with light and dark patches. I slither and inch deeper. I See something. A glow? Is that a color? I feel a flutter in my stomach that reminds me to pay attention to my physical reactions. I pay attention to my eyes. They only slightly burn. I haven't been in long. Good. I have to be faster than I have ever been.

That flutter in my gut was telling me this is it. Color. Of course it would be color. It's Eri. I am looking for the memory of her telling her father about her being an Aurae. She had just lit up the brain. Eri's secret thrust itself at Dr. Kuono in a wave of color at the very moment he pieced together the formula of Extraction. That's why the two memories are fused.

So this is it then. This green and yellow bubbling up through the gray. This colored mass is the conjoined memory. Can I Extract it? Can I grab color?

I slither down a little further. It's warmer here. Like a sun patch in the ocean waves. The heat from Eri's light? The light of the brain, maybe? I spread my fingers as I reach in.

The light is not what I thought. It's not like a ray of light or a laser beam. It's a jellyfish. It's slippery and wants to avoid my grasp. I sink my fingernails into it and grip with everything I have. It resists and sends a stinging, burning sensation through my fingers, into my hands, and up my arms. Add that to the burning eyes. I feel as if I have suddenly burst into flames.

Now that I have what I think is the memory, I realize I have to get back up. I have to get out. I will have to stay straight and long, but I can no longer lead with my arms. I use my legs as a tail and do my best attempt at impersonating a mermaid. I am moving, but I am slow.

My hands feel as though what I am holding is less of a memory and more a glowing ember. At least that is trumping the burn in my eyes.

Do I have it? Do I have the memory? And if I do, what then? Will Luke be able to See and Extract it?

A little further. The thickness around me seems to be separating. I must be almost there.

I don't feel like I have fingers anymore. My hands are oven mitts, only instead of keeping me protected from heat, they are made of fire themselves. I hope that I am still gripping this memory as if my life depends on it, because it does. One last kick, one last bending at the knees, and I feel the edge on the top of my head. I close my eyes and I am out.

I would love to nurse my eyes for a second, to keep them closed, but I don't have time. I need to see his face. Dr. Kuono's face. If the Extraction was successful, I will know immediately. This is not like my other Extractions, where the being did not know I was going in. Dr. Kuono not only knows I was in; he knows what I was after. Now that I am out, he will try to remember the secret of Extraction. He will search his brain. If he no longer knows, I've done it.

I force my eyes open. My eyelids rake over my eyeballs like gritty sandpaper. Everything is pink, but I can see one thing. Dr. Kuono is smiling.

Through a filmy haze I look around the room. Are Luke and Eri okay? A sinking question fills me. Has the room been swarmed with Seer soldiers here to do Tobias's bidding?

But it's still us three. Dr Kuono is fine, better, if I can guess by the expression of relief he wears. Eri is still standing before the brain, although she has let go and the singeing light is now a soft glow. Luke stands at the end of the table now. I squint to be sure, but I don't see Tobias anymore. I make my way over to Luke. A foot from the table, I notice Luke's stance, how hunched he is, that he is straddling something. When I look down, I realize he is straddling the lifeless body of Tobias.

"What *happened*?" I direct my question to Luke. My voice is tight like a clenched fist, and it surprises me. But then I feel the tightness take me over. Why am I angry with Luke for immobilizing the man responsible for all this?

He hears the anger. He must, because his answer is immediately defensive: "You don't know what he was thinking or what he is capable of, Leesie. You don't know what he was going to do to you!" he hisses. He sounds crazed. His eyes, red ringed, are wild with rage.

"How do you know? *What did you do?*" I demand.

"I went in. I Navigated Tobias," he replies more calmly.

"I can see that by your eyes. But that doesn't leave a man in a heap last time I checked, Luke! What did you do?"

"I went in, and the things I saw—" He steps over Tobias, brings his feet together, and stands up straight to look at me.

"I just started taking things, Leesie. Memories. As many as I could hold. I stuffed my hands and arms, and I swam out. I didn't know what else to do. It just came to me. This idea that if I stole enough information, I could—"

"What? Kill him?" I challenge, though I don't know why. I want him dead anyway, so why do I care? Why is this bothering me?

"Tobias is not dead," Dr. Kuono says, moving toward Tobias and bending over him. "He is comatose. The brain is severely damaged, I am sure. But he is not dead."

"Leesie, I had to act," Luke explains. "I had to do something. You needed more time. Eri's distraction provided us seconds, but you needed minutes. It just happened."

It's funny to watch him explain himself to me. He seems to feel the need to explain, almost apologize, for what he did to

Tobias. And he looks confused by it, too. I guess we both have to figure out what it is about this situation that has us uneasy.

But we don't have time to—that's for sure. I need to switch my focus to Eri and her father.

"Are you guys okay?"

"We're okay. You? Did you? Were you able to?" Eri's voice grows more insistent with each question.

"Elise was successful."

Dr. Kuono's voice, even that he has one, that he is a person who knows us, is strange. I have been thinking of him as the neuroscientist for so long. Sure, as Eri's father I wanted to protect him, but I wasn't thinking of him as a living, breathing part of our lives. And now that I see him as such, I am relieved that he's okay. He has been under Tobias's thumb much longer than I have.

"Thank you," he continues, "for risking your life for ours."

"I'm glad it worked. I wasn't sure I could do it," I reply.

"I was. My daughter and Luke have told me about your abilities. You have gained a reputation."

"I know nothing about that. There's so much I don't know."

Dr. Kuono has kind eyes. Full of laugh lines. He smiles and moves closer to me. "You found your way today. You made a selfless choice. You saved me. You saved my daughter, Luke, and all her friends. Even if you never regain your memories, you will make new ones. With people who care about you. You are strong. Trust yourself."

I know that he's right. But I wonder how long it will take for me to be able to put his wise words into practice. The moment between us is gone. Dr. Kuono's eyes refocus, become sharp, and his voice has a new sense of urgency.

"You two must leave," he says. "This laboratory belongs to Seers, to Tobias. It is only a matter of time before someone comes. Elise, you must be on your way to safety by then. Now that you have the joined memory in you, it may have separated. The memory may be readable now. They may be able to Navigate you and See it. You need to be in a safe place before Luke can attempt to Extract it."

He's right. I know he's right. But life is moving so fast today. I want to slow the world down. I want more time with Eri.

Luke and Dr. Kuono begin to discuss the next steps. I listen as he tells Dr. Kuono that his team will be here in minutes to collect Tobias. That Dr. Kuono and Eri are to wait for them. And he and I are going underground.

What? *Underground?* Suddenly I am aware that Luke is part of something much bigger than I have been led to believe.

Eri turns to me and rushes out a whimpering, "Leesie, be careful. I will miss you. I know I will see you again—" Her voice breaks before she can say any more.

Luke is beside me, ushering me to the door.

"Go. Let's go."

I know better than to argue.

We rush out the door, and as I listen to the screeching of his tires peeling from the parking lot, I know that my world is crashing and changing again. My mind is reeling.

"Leesie, it's going to be okay. You'll see."

His voice is soft now, soothing. His voice attempts to convince me that I am heading into an unknown but that this time I travel with someone who cares about me. I want to believe that. I have to believe that.

"How do you know?" I ask, pleading with my eyes for him to settle me down.

"Because you are still alive. You are the only one who houses the formula, the ability to transform Seers into Extractors. And you are the key to ending this. I know you are."

I let his words sink like a weighted hook into murky water. We have completed this mission, and even with the threat of the next mission to get rid of the Preceptors and Extractors working with Tobias, I can't help the flutter in my gut from exploding into a surge of excitement.

With the loss of my past, I have felt so vulnerable and broken. And while the enormity of what I have lost will continue to fragment me, today I have proven that I am also powerful. This part of my life, the part that left me a pawn in the Preceptors' game, is complete. But a new life, a real life for me, is just beginning.